Good Intentions

-Lakinia Ramsey-

"DEFINITION" Copyright © 2010 by Lakinia Ramsey

ebook Edition: Abstract Village, 2013

Print Edition: Abstract Village, 2013

GOOD INTENTIONS / LAKINIA RAMSEY – 1st ed.

ISBN-13: 978-1484844670

ISBN-10: 148484467X

Cover Image: "Image Copyright Vector Ninja 2013 Used under license from Shutterstock.com".

Cover Art and Design: Theopolis and Lakinia Ramsey (Abstract Village)

Dedication

GOD, thank you for it all

For *Theopolis Ramsey* aka "Young Theo" aka "TheOriginal" aka "Thee-Lee"...thank you for choosing me to be your partner in this often insane life. Still standing, unscathed.

Dedication to the Author

A man that hath friends must shew himself friendly: and there is a friend that sticketh closer than a brother. Prov 18:24 KJV

This was somewhat difficult to write especially because my words can't quite encompass how my heart feels about you. You have been a friend, but more than friendship you have been my family. We have shared so many things. We've shared lunch, laughs, tears and even shared a room in Cooooossstttaaaa Riccccaaaaaaa!! Through it all, I have gained so much from you. I will say that you are one of the most genuine, loving and honest people that I have had the privilege of knowing.

To say I'm proud is an understatement. If you get to know someone you see the gifts that God places in them and your heart's desire for them is that they use those gifts to bless others. This my friend, is going to be a blessing to so many people.

I could go on and on about how wonderful you are, but again unless you are able to read my heart then you can't quite understand the love that I have for you. Thank you my sister, my friend, my confidante, my road dog and my shoulder on so many occasions. You epitomize true friendship and I'm glad that our paths crossed. If I've never said before how much you truly mean to me, today let me say that my life would not be the same if you weren't a part of it. I am better for knowing you…

I love you to infinity BFFFFTTTTTT!

PS: Thank you for letting me raise your son ;)

Reshunda
aka
Sweet Baby Rae !!

Acknowledgments

Completing this book has definitely been an adventure, which can be numerous in this journey of life. For this adventure, for this incredible life, for the gift of words I thank HIM. For strength, for perseverance, for courage, I thank HIM.

I will also take this opportunity to express my heartfelt gratitude to some very important, first-class people.

Theopolis (Theo) Ramsey you are the most amazing husband. I thank you for being supportive, for being my strength, for reading drafts at 4 o'clock in the morning, for making 1000 cups of coffee, for holding down the fort while I was on a "break". Love is love, love.

My mom, Doshia Watts who has always encouraged me to dream bigger than my circumstances. To my pops, James O. Watts who gave me the love for art and music.

My sister Yasmin Watts, thank you for always being there…you are beautiful and smart, thank you for being you and for giving birth to my nephew Camden, who without his light, I would have never found my way out of my darkest hours.

To my fantastic Pit Crew: Theo, my brother Zach Watts, Porscha Armour, my "sister" Melissa Robinson, for being my support system, my creative team, and my editors. Zach, you will always be my baby boy.

To my grandparents, Rev. Arthur Watts, and Minnie "Francis" Mitchell, who taught me the true meaning of unconditional love. Your spirits reside within me always.

To my uncles, the first "loves" of my life, and always my guardians: Eddie Mitchell, Clarence Mitchell, Roosevelt Mitchell, Willie Mitchell, Clyde Mitchell (RIP), Lee Mitchell (RIP), Charlie Mitchell Jr.(RIP)

To my cousin, sister and best friend: Shaquita Mitchell, wow, look at us…we've come a long way from our first little apartment in Cripple Creek.

To my unsung heroes, William and Tonya Ramsey, you have always been my inspiration and my motivation.

To my "babies", even though I did not birth you, I carry a small piece of every single one of you with me. You give me life: Ryan "R Double" Ramsey, Montez "Dirty" Smith, Bontavia "Ban"Anderson, Edwina "Ed" Price, Erica "E Walk" Walker., Kortney "KoJo" Johnson, Natasha "Libra" Winston, Terri "Loubabee" Lewis, Curtis "Curt" Rodgers., Roderick "Jamere" Morgan, Eden and Rory Edge, Shavon "Von" Deriso, LaNorris Sawyer, Crystal "Becky" Ramsey, Toris Ramsey, Chris Ramsey, Saire Ramsey

To my family (Watts, Thomas, Mitchell, Ramsey, Deriso…), thank you for carrying me and keeping me.

To my absolutely awesome friends, even that word seems too mundane for who you are to me: Reshunda Gresham., Darien Major, Simone Major, Venus Griffin, Amelia Biggs, Temo Supremo (Melissa Barragan, Gabby Barragan, Kameyan Sims), Matee Brisbane, Nicole Jenkins and so many others…you have been there at my best and my worst, you never let me give up, and most importantly, you take me and love me exactly as I am.

To my honorable brothers of distinction, Alpha Phi Alpha (Mu Delta Chapter)…I love me some you. (RIP Marvin F. Wilson)

To my Woodall Family, past and present…I love you and thanks for being EVERYTHING.

To anyone and everyone who has ever pushed, pulled, encouraged, enlightened, listened, motivated, inspired…thank you and I love you.

GOD Bless.

Table of Contents

"*Hell isn't merely paved with good intentions; it's walled and roofed with them. Yes, and furnished too.*"

- Aldous Huxley

GOOD INTENTIONS

-Reflections, Toni Charles

Everyone has these moments. Moments when you take a deep breath, take an assessment of your life, and wonder how in the hell you ended up just where you are. That's exactly the place where I am in my life right now. Alone, thinking back to all of the life choices that brought me to this place. Not that I'm looking for pity. I didn't exactly fall into the situation I'm now facing. On second thought, I did fall…fell head over heels in love with another woman's husband…landed so far away from my own truth and reality that I almost couldn't recognize the person I faced in the mirror anymore. Then again, such is life. Just when you think you have it all figured out…a storm comes along and disrupts it, leaving ruin and chaos in its wake. For me, that disruptive force of nature came in the form of Keenan Jackson.

Chapter 1: The Story of Us

My city: Atlanta. There is a reason that it's called "Hotlanta". When the summertime rolls around, it's *the* hottest place to be. Summer concerts and festivals, jazz in the parks, clubs banging…people hanging. The city becomes an illustration of life in motion… the lovers, the mothers, the beautiful, fine brothers… even those homeless on the corners. The city is a complex mixture of beauty and grittiness…elements that I have come to love over the past years.

....

It's Saturday morning and I'm on my way downtown to meet with two of my closest friends, Rayna "Rae" Williams and Dawn DeVoe, at Café Intermezzo on the infamous Peachtree Street. Thankfully, it is not as humid as it can typically get around this time of year. Still seasonably hot, but the presence of a slight breeze has decreased the intensity. As a rule, we have met every Saturday for breakfast or brunch; however, our lives have gotten so busy with work and family that we have settled with meeting on alternate Saturdays. These occasions are essential, our moments to vent, cry, laugh, or whatever it is we need to do to put us back on track to surviving in the real world.

Rae has been my best friend since my years at Georgia State University. When I first moved to Atlanta, I was the stereotypical, terrified small-town girl, who had big dreams of working and living in the city. My friends were few and my money even less. My only family in the area was my aunt Shana, my mother's youngest sister. At the time, Shana was a seemingly mature twenty-three while I was a naive eighteen, dynamics that enabled her to have a great impact on the molding of my social life.

....

Living in Atlanta has provided me with opportunities that I never thought were possible. I grew up in a small Georgia town…at least a three-hour drive from the city. For most locals, dreams consisted of graduating from high school, marrying, finding a good job, usually at one of the numerous factories, and living a decent life. Some went to college, but even those who ventured out found themselves back home again at some point. My dreams were bigger than that. I felt stifled by the town's boundaries. Stifled by the limited opportunities. So, one week after graduation, I moved in with Shana, me and my two suitcases. My only regret was leaving my father. As the only child of him and my mother, I felt a sense of obligation to stay, to take care of him; my mother, having long since abandoned those duties. But he urged me to go, to get a taste of another life. He was unselfish that way. So now here I am, in this city that is three hours away from home, yet seemingly in another world.

Life here has been good. Since I've been here I've been partying at the hottest clubs, eating at the trendiest restaurants, and I've been meeting, and sometimes dating, the most beautiful people. Under Shana's tutelage, I became the ultimate social butterfly; learning how to dress, wear my hair, and how to network. Yet, even though I became known as her protégé, at heart I have never felt like the socialite she groomed me to be. For me, the culture of the city, and not the social scene, is its biggest inspiration. Of course I go to parties, but I am always trying to make new connections for my artistic passions. I've always believed that the true gems of the city are not to be found in its club scene, but in its museums, at its spoken word events, at its exhibits and art shows.

....

Atlanta's underground culture of art and music served as the backdrop to my first introduction to Rae. The first poetry event I attended was at this small coffee shop named Black Moon Café. Greg Moran, a close friend and host of the event, invited me to perform. Because it was my first time reading in front of a large crowd, I was noticeably nervous. Rae, who was one of the other artists performing that night, helped to put me at ease. Instantly we bonded, a rare occurrence between me and females.

As I watched her perform her piece that night, I was taken aback at this petite, yet vibrant young sister who filled the space with her powerful voice and emotional words. She spoke about all-too familiar themes in the lives of women… love lost, love gone wrong, cheating and betrayal. Rae stood on the stage with her eyes closed… her heart flowing fluidly through her words like tears. I found myself crying with her, not knowing her story, but understanding her song. After that night we became the best of friends.

I soon discovered that poetry wasn't the only thing we had in common. Rae was also a struggling student at Georgia State. She is from Atlanta though, so for her it less of an adjustment. Taking me under her wings, she guided me through the exploits of college life, introducing me to her countless friends and dragging me to parties. It was at one of those infamous parties that I met the person who would become my other best friend, Kyle Jordan.

With Rae's influence, I was able to get a job waitressing at Houston's, one of Atlanta's more popular restaurants. During the day, we attended classes… at night we balanced studying with our demanding work schedules. Eventually, I started spending less time at Shana's and more time sleeping on Rae's couch in her one bedroom apartment in the West End. It wasn't the safest spot in the city, but it was affordable and a short commute to the college. Besides, on any given day, at least one of Rae's three brothers made random appearances as if they were our personal bodyguards.

....

My evolving relationship with Rae would come to be a welcomed distraction from my slowly disintegrating relationship with Shana. Although my mom and I had a strained relationship, my relationship with Shana has always been a close one. That is until she unknowingly became the cause of my first heartbreak when she slept with Greg Moran.

I loved Greg. Initially we were just friends, but our friendship developed into more. He was always promoting events and anytime I wasn't performing, I would volunteer as his assistant. Even though he was older, and had already graduated, we spent a lot of time together. He was handsome, charming, creative, temperamental...characteristics I came to love. But I never told him because I wasn't sure that he loved me back. There were definitely moments when I felt a strong bond between us, but there were other moments when he seemed distant. I just chalked it up to him being a moody artist. Our relationship ultimately evolved into a sexual one, yet there was no pretense that we were exclusive. Even though I knew that Greg had other girls, he was my one. Naively, I waited, yearning for something more. It never happened. Rae always tried to warn me. From the beginning, she never trusted Greg. But I was 19, and blinded by love...or maybe lust.

My fantasy came to an abrupt end one night after one of the events. Shana and some of her friends came out as a show of support. I was excited for the chance for her to finally meet Greg. Because of our questionable status, I only introduced him as close friend. They hit it off immediately. I was ecstatic. That was until the next morning when I ran into a half-naked Greg when I fumbled my way into the kitchen to make my routine pot of coffee. Embarrassed, he just stood there staring at me. I was too numb to be angry or jealous. If anything, I was disappointed that he wasn't the man I wanted him to be.

After numerous apologies and conversations, Greg and I still tried to maintain our friendship, but the dynamics had been irreparably tainted. It wasn't long before my relationship with Shana also changed. Even though we never talked about Greg, the situation became tense. I don't know if he ever told her about us or whether or not she just sensed it, as women often do, but I could tell that she wasn't comfortable with us being around each other. I became determined to spend less time at the apartment. In doing so, I spent more time at Rae's before ultimately deciding to move in. The space was cramped, but we made it work and we had fun in the process. We lived in that apartment for two years before we graduated, got better jobs, and just like George and Weezy, moved on up.

....

Deciding to still live together after graduation, we rented a three-bedroom townhouse in Southwest Atlanta. There we lived until I had saved enough money to put a down payment on my first house. After divorcing her husband, Dawn moved into the townhouse with Rae, along with her five year old daughter Alexis, or as we affectionately call her, "Lexie". And that is the condensed story of us.

Finally, I pulled up to the restaurant and hurried out of the car. As usual, I was running late and so I prepared myself for the grief I would get from the both of them. My tardiness is never intentional; however, time always has a habit of getting away from me.

I looked around, spotting Rae and Dawn at our customary table in the corner overlooking the street. We come here often enough that the waiters and the owner know us on a first name basis. The staff, the décor, the food, the overall atmosphere of the restaurant make it one of our favorites. Walking to the table, I could already tell by the look on their faces that I was about to get a mean lecture about being late. It wouldn't be anything that I hadn't heard before. Undaunted, I headed to the table, anticipating their speeches.

"Hey chick, I would tell you good-morning, but the morning is almost over or did you happen to notice?" Rae was the first to complain, but I laughed away her mood, "Well good morning ladies, I love your beautiful attitudes to go along with this beautiful morning."

"Oh you know I have an attitude," Dawn chimed in. "Please explain to me how I always manage to arrive before you when I not only have myself, but a daughter to feed, bathe, and dress?"

"Whatever," I rolled my eyes "I did not get out of bed just to get drilled by you heifers. My life is stressful enough during the week. I'm here and that's all that matters."

"Well we've been waiting on you so hurry up and figure out what you want to order because I'm starving" stated Rae.

Even though I normally order the same meal, I made a big production of looking over the menu. It was a personal source of amusement to see Rae's face turn varying shades of red with her growing impatience. Rae's appetite is legendary among our circle of friends, while also being a source of mystery. No one can figure out where she manages to store all of the food she consumes in her petite body. I, on the other hand, am on the complete opposite end of the spectrum. I can easily gain weight just by staring at a cookie long enough.

Gradually, the attitudes dissipated as we started rehashing a week's worth of drama over omelets, fruit dishes, and fried potatoes. Dawn and I listened as Rae briefed us on an intense, escalating situation she was having at work. Recently, she had received a promotion to Senior Associate at her marketing firm. Although she was able to celebrate her good fortune with us, she did not have the privilege of sharing it with her fellow co-workers. Unfortunately, she had to deal with "haters" on the job who were spreading rumors that she was sleeping her way up the corporate ladder. One co-worker in particular, Monica Dawson, had been vying for the job and as a result of the promotion, had been making Rae's life a living hell.

Dawn was having baby daddy issues as usual. Jamie, her ex-husband, was supposed to be getting Lexie for the summer, but, as was becoming his habitual manner, he was trying to cancel at the last minute. Dawn had become beyond frustrated with his antics. She was sick and tired of him not being responsible for the child that they both had a hand in creating. The crazy thing is, when they were married, Jamie could have won the "father of the year" award. It was a rare occurrence to see him without Lexie near his side. If she became sick at school, it was Jamie who would take time off from work to care for her. He relished any time that he was able to spend with his baby girl. Once he and Dawn divorced, however, it was as if the divorce decree included Lexie too. He either showed up late at planned family events or just didn't show up at all.

As for me, well, my problem was the same as always…too much work and definitely not enough play. Two years ago, I became the proud co-owner of Muse, a café/bookstore, with another girlfriend, Tanya Jones. For years we had talked about opening up our own place. We always believed it would come to fruition, however, we never imagined it would be this soon. It wasn't all without hard work, dedication, and education though. We had to do our due diligence in researching the market before starting an account to cover the down payment on a venue and the other start-up costs of a new venture.

Our fortunes changed one night when we attended a networking event and happened to meet Daniel Moore, a sexy brother with a big smile and, as we later discovered, even bigger pockets. Daniel was well connected in the Atlanta area. He was a broker at a local firm, and also a member of an investment group that was always looking for ways to invest back into the black community. To Daniel, our concept of the store was refreshing and revitalizing, because, as he put it, too many black folk were trying to start music studios or restaurants that all too often closed shop before the ink was even dry on the final paperwork.

After the event, Daniel took us under his wing and helped us to develop our business plan. In a year's time, we had enough funds to cover salaries for the both of us and for the start-up costs. We found a nice space to lease in midtown Atlanta and two years ago, Muse had its official grand opening. Daniel is not only a partner, he's also proven to be a valuable asset. The journey has not been an easy one, but we have worked hard to develop the business, our image and our clientele.

Most of my free time is spent at the store, mainly handling the marketing aspects of the business, while Tanya handles the management responsibilities. I develop and promote events, while always looking for ways to expand our primary base. It's an inside joke that I'm always "on" because even when I'm not at the store, I'm always hunting down new artists, new opportunities, and new connections. The problem is the fact that even though I attend a lot of social events, I have never really found the time or the energy to develop any meaningful relationships with guys. I have met a lot of intelligent and ambitious brothers, but a single girl has to be careful on the Atlanta dating scene. Unfortunately, the rumors are more fact than fiction. It's true that there are a lot of "down-low" brothers, out and proud brothers and brothers who are taking advantage of the "good man shortage" by trying to be *that* man to about ten different sisters. Then, there are the brothers who just can't seem to handle being in a relationship with a strong, successful black woman. Still, some good brothers have come across my path, but I just can't seem to find that special connection with any one man who can keep me interested in the relationship. So I'll usually date a guy for a hot minute, and then use the demands of the business as my escape route out of the relationship.

Rae and Dawn constantly tease me about loving the idea of love more so than the reality of it. Maybe so. That's not an uncommon Libra characteristic. Even so, I still believe that there has to be a brother our there waiting to blow my mind with his intelligence, his beauty, and yes, his sex. There is absolutely nothing wrong with wanting the total package and I am willing to wait for him if I have to.

We continued to discuss our life issues until the conversation switched to possibilities for tonight's agenda. Luckily, Dawn had her freedom since her cousin Traci had graciously agreed to babysit Lexie. After a brief discussion, we decided to have a girl's night at my house, something we have not managed to accomplish in an eternity. After air kisses and hugs, we left the restaurant with the idea that we would meet up again at my house at 8 o'clock.

Chapter 2: From the Shadows

I awoke with a start…realizing that my alarm was ringing incessantly. I was dismayed to discover that it was already 7:30 p.m., meaning that I would probably be unprepared when Dawn and Rae arrived. Quickly, I jumped out of bed and headed straight for the shower. Once out, I grabbed the most comfortable pair of shorts I could find and a white tee. I pulled my hair into a puffy ponytail and surveyed the effects. My reflection was almost identical to the college version of myself, which I guess is a good thing. I have always been told that I am a beautiful woman; nevertheless, I recognize that my beauty is not traditional. I am not the thin, fair-skinned, long-haired version of the black woman that my black men and society in general seemed to favor. I'm barely over five feet tall, my hair is a shock of natural curls, and my skin is the color of the mocha coffee drinks that are my passion.

....

I rushed to the kitchen to arrange an assortment of chips and dips on a tray. The ladies were bringing hot wings and pizza from Manny's, a neighborhood restaurant that Rae and I use to frequent when we lived together. Heinekens were put in a cooler on ice, butter-cream scented candles were lit, and the "girl's night" movie collection was in place, including my all-time favorite, *Love Jones*. After reviewing my stash, I realized that I needed to add *The Best Man* to the mix. While Rae and Dawn have been drawn to the tall and handsome brothers like Boris Kodjoe, my favorites have always included the brown-skinned "shorties" like Larenz Tate and Taye Diggs.

The DVD player had just been set when the doorbell rang. I hurried to open the door since Dawn was one to ring the doorbell relentlessly until someone answered. When I opened the door, there she stood, greeting me with a wide grin plastered on her face. Like mine, her long hair was pulled into a ponytail. Unpredictably, she wore a long-sleeved tee and sweats. Being that this was a sleepover I should have expected that; however she is such a diva that it wouldn't have surprised me at all if she had arrived in makeup and heels. As she came in, her unsteady strut across the floor confirmed what I already suspected, that she had a few before her arrival. Following close behind her was Rae, geared in pink pajamas, who went straight to the kitchen to unload the pizzas and wings. To get the party in gear, I turned on the smooth, sexy sounds of John Legend. Dawn grabbed me and we began singing and slow dancing, both of us fantasizing that the other person was the man of our dreams. Rae joined us, bringing some beers with her. I popped mine and without much thought, took a long swig in my first attempt to erase all of my frustrations of the week.

We danced and laughed for a while, before I finally got around to putting in *The Best Man*, beginning our movie marathon. As the movie started, Dawn announced that she had bumped into Kyle. I was excited to get the news that Kyle was back in town. For the past month he had been in D.C. tying up some loose ends after the death of his mother from breast cancer. Kyle and I have always been close. The "street committee" defined us as lovers, but truthfully, we are more like brother and sister. That's not to say that he wouldn't be a great candidate. Kyle was extremely handsome...tall with a gorgeous smile, skin the color of caramel. An up and coming attorney with a prestigious law firm, he already owned his own home, and drove a brand new BMW. However...he was also a "pretty boy" and after Greg, "pretty boys" were no longer my type. There was also his persistent problem with fidelity. With so many women constantly throwing themselves at him, it was a struggle for him to remain faithful to one woman. He was not unaware of the fact that he was a hot commodity and like any hot blooded male, he enjoyed all of the perks that afforded him.

The more I thought about him being back, the more curious I was that he hadn't called me. I let it go, confident that in time he would call whenever his life settled down.

We were in the right middle of an argument over who was the finest Taye Diggs, or Terrence Howard, when the doorbell rang again. This surprised me because I wasn't expecting anyone.

As I looked through the keyhole, my face beamed with recognition. I snatched the door open and jumped right into Kyle's waiting arms. He laughed, while struggling to maintain his balance. "Dang girl, you missed me huh?"

I laughed also, still hugging him close. "You know I did baby, I was about to be mad at you when Dawn told us that you were in town and I hadn't heard from you." Promptly, he apologized, explaining that not only had he just gotten back, but his cousin came back with him and he was trying to help him get settled.

It was then that I noticed movement from the shadows of the yard. As Kyle began introducing me to his cousin Keenan Jackson, I had to catch my breath when he started walking closer to the door. To say the brother was fine was an understatement. He was my idea of beautiful. His skin the color of mahogany… his smile, gorgeous, accentuated by a dimple in his right cheek. He had mid-length dreads that were pulled back into a ponytail and a goatee that was trimmed to perfection. Even in the dimly lit doorway, I could see his defined muscles beyond the t-shirt and jeans he was wearing. *Have mercy.*

I was still trying to compose myself when Keenan smiled and reached out his hand in greeting. "Toni, it's good to finally meet you. I've heard a lot about you from Kyle." The voice was smooth, definitely with an upstate accent.

"Nice to finally meet you too Keenan." *Keenan.* Over the years I've heard his name mentioned on several occasions. Kyle's cousin, who was like a brother to him. Although we never had a chance to meet, I knew from my conversations with Kyle that they grew up having an extremely close bond.

Moving aside, I invited them into my home. As expected, Rae's eyes peaked with interest when Keenan stepped inside of the doorway. As Kyle made introductions, I could see her trying desperately to get my attention. Immediately she had recognized that Keenan was my type. I announced that I was going to refill snacks and snatched up the empty trays on my way to the kitchen. I didn't have to look to know that Rae was following close behind me. As soon as we got into the kitchen she started.

"Girl, I was wondering why you were outside for so long, but now I see why. This guy is hot!"

"Rae don't start. I met the brother for all of two minutes and you're already clowning in my kitchen. You're acting like I'm desperate or something."

"I'm not saying you're desperate, I'm just saying this is one hell of an opportunity that has practically fallen into your lap and you know I'm not always fond of your opportunities."

I rolled my eyes at her while shoving bags of chips in her chest. Yeah I was attracted to Keenan, but I didn't know anything about him, and the last thing I needed or wanted was to start something that could complicate matters between me and Kyle. I had seen first-hand with Shana and Greg how quickly situations could become more than uncomfortable. The man, I was interested in, but I definitely was not interested in the drama.

At some point, we managed to make our way back into the living room. Obviously Keenan was having no problems adjusting. He was stretched out on my chaise lounge, his Timberland boots already kicked off and carelessly strewn across the floor. He was laughing at Kyle and Dawn, who were involved in a heated debate over whether or not Taye Digg's character should have told Morris Chestnut's character about sleeping with his soon-to-be wife. His laugh was full, deep…rich. I loved it. Mentally I scolded myself for being easily affected by some guy I barely knew.

Keenan and Kyle's appearance was an invasion on our girl's night, but we had no problems allowing them to stay. We had old-school fun, watching movies, playing board games, and talking about everything and anything that came up for discussion. It was as if we had known Keenan forever. Throughout the night, there were times he would catch me watching him and I would instantly look away, embarrassed. Yeah I was definitely feeling him.

The guys ultimately left around 3 a.m. I promised Kyle that I would call him next week so we could set up a lunch date. Keenan hugged me before he left and I almost lost myself in his embrace. I watched them walk towards Kyle's car. Before getting in, Keenan looked back and we made eye contact. This time I didn't look away. He stared back…then he smiled. *Trouble.*

Chapter 3: Gravity

The week flew by, which proved to be a blessing because it gave me very little time to think about Keenan. We had to prepare for a spoken word contest we were hosting, a huge event for local college students and many local artists. The cash prize was a $5000 scholarship, with most of the money being raised through fundraisers. I was becoming more and more excited about the work we were doing. As promised, we were not just a business trying to make a profit. We were actually making an impact in the community.

As sponsors, we are not supposed to be biased towards any of the artists. Nevertheless, I certainly had my favorite. Secretly, I was rooting for Mia Scott, a 19 year old college student at our alma mater, Georgia State. A talented artist, she had been a featured performer at several of our events. Our bond developed when she was preparing to perform at her first event. She reminded me so much of my shy, younger self so I tried to be a comforting voice, like Rae was to me during my initiation. After the performance, she became a regular at Muse, either hanging out or volunteering for events. We spent a lot of time together and after numerous discussions, I discovered that she came from a broken home rampant with abuse. Estranged from her family, she was diligently working to make her way through college on her own. Initially, I was her mentor but, over time, I became more like her big sister. Muse became her refuge from the world.

On the night of the event, Tanya had the honor of announcing the winner. When I heard Mia's name, I was glad that it was Tanya on the stage and not myself, as I could barely contain my enthusiasm. Afterwards, we closed the store and had an official celebration party. Mia was glowing and I knew this was only the beginning of big things in store for her.

....

Regrettably, with such a busy week, Kyle and I never had the opportunity to meet for lunch. Once, we briefly spoke and it was obvious that he was really stressed out from trying to get back into the flow with his job. During our conversation, he mentioned that he was helping Keenan move into a new apartment. I could only laugh nervously when he playfully suggested that he may have to dump him off on me for a day or two. The thought of seeing him again sent shivers of excitement running through me; however, I did not want Kyle to sense that. He, being an attorney granted him almost supernatural powers of perception. I simply told him to let me know if he needed me and after a short conversation we hung up.

....

On Saturday mornings when I'm not at Intermezzo, I'm usually at Muse bright and early. Even though we don't officially open until 10 a.m., I've established a routine of going in, making coffee, reading, or simply watching the city wake up from its slumber. Years of living with my grandmother trained me to be an early bird. During the week, I get to the store around 7 a.m. and watch the steady stream of corporate employees hurriedly make their way to their respective offices. They scurry out of parking decks and MARTA stations, dressed in trendy suits, paired with sneakers in preparation for their long walks. Cell phones attached to their ears like extended appendages.

The mornings are often quiet. Most of the traffic comes from a steady stream of college students, wandering couples, or others like Mia, looking for a safe place to hide away from the world. The first taste of my second cup of coffee was still lingering on my tongue when a now familiar face walked up to the glass door. He lightly tapped. At first, the force of gravity would not enable me to cross the room in order to allow Keenan Jackson access to my world. As I sat staring…he stood there smiling. Unhurriedly, I stood up and went to unlock the door.

....

Keenan Jackson walked into my store and I could no longer lie to myself about my attraction to him. This morning, his dreads were loose, falling across his shoulders. Again, he had on a T-Shirt with a pair of jeans, but sneakers now replaced the boots he previously wore.

I was the first to speak, "Hey Keenan, I'm surprised to see you."

"What's up Toni? I'm sorry to catch you off guard, but Kyle told me about your store so since I was up early I decided to come check it out. I hope you don't mind."

Do I mind your fine ass coming to see me? Hell no. "Of course not. The store's not officially open, but I get here early to have coffee. Would you like some? I just made a fresh pot."

He accepted. I went to pour him a cup while he checked out some of the newest arrivals. Secretly, I stole glances of him as he walked around.

"Do you take cream and sugar?"

"Yes" he smiled, "a little cream, a whole lotta sugar."

Lord that smile. I took his coffee, along with a coaster, and set it down next to mine at the booth I had been occupying. He followed me to the booth and sat down. I tried to make easy conversation, if nothing more than to slow down my escalating heart rate.

"So…did you have a good time last weekend?" Instantly he smiled that gorgeous smile.

"I did. I did. I appreciate you allowing me to hang out."

"Well hopefully we can hang out again before you leave." This was my attempt to find out just how long he would be in town.

"Well…I've been here with Kyle for a couple of weeks now and I'm really drawn to Atlanta…the people, the city…I've made some good connections so I may be here for a minute." *Exactly what I wanted to hear.*

I questioned him about the connections he was trying to make and immediately became captivated with his story when he told me that he was an artist. Apparently, he had reached a stalemate in D.C. and Kyle convinced him to move to Atlanta for a fresh start. He inquired about Muse and somehow, I found myself opening up to this almost stranger about my life journey from the country to the city. I explained how early in my career, I realized that my passion was not in being a 9 to 5 employee. He laughed, explaining that he had worked as an associate in a marketing firm, before deciding to trade in the time clock to become a full-time artist. Most of his friends and family thought he was absolutely insane, but he realized that you couldn't put a price tag on freedom. Of course, I completely understood his sentiments. It felt really good to finally have a conversation with someone who *got it*. When the thought of opening Muse was still just a dream on paper, Dawn thought I was crazy for wanting to become an entrepreneur at such a young age. In her mind, it was just easier to get a steady paycheck and let someone else have the headaches of running the business. From the beginning though, Rae always supported me. She knew that I was a free spirit who could never be content with corporate constraints.

We continued to talk, to laugh, to share. Regrettably, I realized that it was almost time to open up shop. I did not want our conversation to end. I was really, really feeling him and my intuition led me to believe that he was feeling me too. I presented him with an open invitation to hang out as long as he liked, but he said he could only have one more cup of coffee before he had to head back out to finish some errands. I wanted to give him my cell number, but the last thing I wanted to do was to appear desperate. I couldn't stress about it much longer as a few customers filed in through the now open doors. As I was speaking to a young sister who was looking for a steamy summer read, Keenan caught my attention, pointed to the door, and smiled as he headed out. I gave him a small wave, and cursed myself for being a coward. I hated to see him leave, but he definitely left a great impression as he walked away.

Chapter 4: PDA (Public Display of Affection)

It was unusually busy all day, but there was no way that I was going to complain about it. The more business, the more money. Tanya came in around 2 p.m. so when she got settled, I seized the opportunity to take a small break. Grabbing a cup of coffee, I headed to the office to call Dawn to see if she had a plan for the night. It took several rings before she groggily answered.

"Dawn, wake up. I know you're not still sleeping. How is that even possible when you have a five year old kid? Don't you have some cartoons to watch or some pancakes to make?"

"Girl, shut-up. Don't hate on me because I have a life and you decided to become Ms. Fortune 500. Besides, Traci kept Lexie while I went out last night. Are you still at the store?"

"Yeah I am. Tanya just came in so I may be able to leave a little early. I'm trying to find out if anything is going on tonight. I'm stressed, I need something good." Of course, as soon as I mentioned going out, she instantly perked up.

"Girl, let me make some calls and get back with you. I heard that some celebrity is supposed to be at Visions plus I know a guy that can get us in VIP. I will just have to sweet talk Traci into keeping Lexie for another night." She revealed that Kyle had called her as well, looking to hang out. My mind directly strayed to Keenan, but I chose not disclose his visit. She and I are close, but that was a conversation I needed to have with Rae. Dawn continued to ramble on for a few minutes about some other events she had heard about. I told her to give me a call back when she had something solid, but I needed to speak to Rae before she got off of the phone. As lazy as she is, she told me to call Rae on her cell phone because she wasn't getting out of bed anytime soon.

....

After hanging up with Dawn, I called Rae to fill her in on the morning details involving Keenan. She was just as surprised as I was about his visit. I admitted to her how attracted I was to him, and my dilemma between wanting to get to know him better and not wanting to cause a rift in my relationship with Kyle. She tried to reason with me by assuring me that Kyle would not hold it against me if I tried to pursue "something" with Keenan. She insisted that he would want both of us to be happy and to just have fun. She also reminded me that Keenan and I were grown and didn't actually need anyone's permission to do "grown folk business." Her statement made me laugh and I was glad that we were able to have this conversation. As always, I could always count on Rae to help me clear my head.

....

I left around 4 o'clock and headed straight home. Dawn called and confirmed that we would definitely be going to Visions. Contact had already been made with Kyle, who told her that he and Keenan would meet us there. Exciting news. There would only be a space of a few hours between our last moments together, but admittedly, I was ready to see him again. Maybe if we were in each other's presence, I could determine if our chemistry was actually real or just imagined on my part. Unfortunately, Rae wasn't going with us because she had other plans. Her mom had planned a family night and demanded that she and her brothers attend. When Mama Ann made a request, she was not to be denied. Rae certainly inherited her stubborn characteristics from her.

It almost frightened me to know that I would be on my own to deal with these out of control emotions, but somehow I would make it through.

....

Once I arrived at home, I tried taking a nap. However, my body was too wired so my efforts proved to be in vain. Instead, I decided to take a bath hoping the warm water and lavender scents would serve to ease my tensions. My aching legs felt relieved when I encased my body in the steamy, bubbly water. Longingly, I wished that I had a partner to massage the knots in my shoulders. As much as I don't want the perceived burdens of a relationship, there are times when my mind drifts with thoughts on how my life could be enriched by having someone at home…waiting to share my life, waiting to love away any stress, fears, or burdens that may assault me in a given day. But there is no lover...only my own flesh and bones to occupy this oversized tub. Frustrated, I finished my bath. Still dripping wet, I walked into my bedroom to get my robe.

Still tense, I fixed a steaming cup of chamomile tea with lemon, which finally helped me to relax. I decided to watch television until it was time for me to get dressed. Visions was in close proximity to my house so it wouldn't take long for me to drive over. It also wouldn't take long for me to get dressed for the night. I wasn't one of those females who took hours to decide on wardrobe, makeup, and hairstyles. I searched the contents of my closet. After reviewing my choices, I decided on a pair of dark jeans, a silver halter top, and completed the look with silver bangles and a pair of high-heeled sandals. I pulled my hair into a carefree, yet sexy ponytail, brushed on some eye shadow and mascara, and glossed my full lips. Glancing in the mirror I prayed that I was sexy enough to pull Keenan's attention since he was the only man that I would be vying for tonight.

....

My excitement and nervousness intensified, as I got near the club. It had been months since I had last been out, leaving me anxious to see what the scene was like. Luckily, Dawn was on a first name basis with half of the security guards in Atlanta, so we are always privileged to enjoy some of the hottest parties and some of the most luxurious VIP sections. I'm not generally a party girl, however, I always make an effort to put my best face forward since I never know who I am going to meet and what new connections I could possibly make. So I tolerate the most obnoxious, flirt with the most hideous, and fake it with the most pretentious, all in the name of good business. Fortunately, Atlanta has a very diverse mix of people from varying ethnicities, cultures, and lifestyles so the nightlife is rarely boring and there's typically some A or B list celebrity making an appearance. I've gotten quite a few gigs lined up at Muse from the connections I've made at different bars, lounges, and clubs. The scene works out great for me on a professional note, personally… well that's another story.

....

I called Dawn before getting out of my car. She answered on the first ring and said that she was just pulling into the club's parking lot. I hung up after receiving instructions to meet her at the door. After checking my makeup, I took a deep breath, and got out of the car. My nerves were getting the best of me. I planned to order a drink as soon as I got inside, hoping to take the edge off. My goal was to have a good buzz going by the time Kyle and Keenan showed up. As I approached the door, I could see that Dawn was already working her charmed magic, smiling that dazzling smile of hers at this tall, sculpted security officer, who stood guarding the door like a Doberman. She was her usual stunning self. Her long hair hung to her shoulders in soft waves. Her long legs were poured into a pair of skinny black jeans. She wore a red off-the-shoulder shirt with strategic cuts that high-lighted her abs. I shook my head. Mr. Security Officer didn't stand a chance. When I got close enough, she grabbed my hand and introduced me.

"Hey girl, this is Mike, Mike, Toni." I extended my hand watching intently as it was engulfed by his massive one. Mike barely glanced my way before turning his full attention back to Dawn. She told him that the two of us were going in, but she had two other friends that would be joining us later. Mike pulled two wristbands out of his back pocket and meticulously attached them to our wrists before ushering us in. This instigated a wave of dirty stares from the people still waiting to be let in, especially the females. We rushed in, heading straight to the VIP section, leaving Mike to defend himself.

Thankfully, it wasn't long before a server showed up to get our drink orders. I ordered a Jack and coke mix while Dawn ordered an amaretto sour. When the server came back, she informed us that our drinks were the courtesy of this handsome brother lounging on one of the leather couches in the back. We smiled and raised our drinks at him in a gesture of thanks. He tilted his head to the side and raised one eyebrow as if to say, "That's it?" Dawn laughed and I realized that the brother wasn't as much of a stranger as I initially believed.

"Ok Dawn, who is Mr. Wanna-Be Baller, already paying for drinks before the club even gets jumping good." A coy smile played on her lips. "Girl I met him here a few weeks ago when I was out with Sheree. Hell I stayed on the floor half of the night with him. That brother has moves."

"Ok…Well you need to go over there and calm Stalker down because he looks like he's going to sit there and stare you down until you say something to him."

She paused momentarily before agreeing, "Yeah, you're right. I guess I need to speak, but I am not here to be tied down to one man. I hope Stalker is on the same page." As she got up and sauntered over to where he was seated, I could almost feel the heat radiating from the brother's eyes as he deliberately gazed up and down her long, lean body. The way he was gawking at her, I didn't think she would be returning anytime soon.

No longer interested, I turned my attention back to my drink and started swaying my body to the beat of the music. I recognized the song as the latest release by Common, a hip-hop artist who was finally getting the recognition he deserved. I was finishing my drink and was prepared to order another one when a hand brushed against the back of my neck. Instantaneously, a jolt of electricity traveled down the length of my spine. I jerked around to see the man who was bold enough to be hitting my spot. As I wheeled around, I found myself gazing directly into Keenan's gorgeous face. I stared for a minute still trying to catch my breath from his touch. He spoke as I attempted to recover.

"Damn, Toni, sorry I startled you" he laughed. *Ohhh that laugh.* I nervously laughed back, trying to act as if I wasn't as affected as I actually was. He surprised me by moving in closer to embrace me. In that instant, his masculine scent assailed my nostrils awakening all of my senses.

"Hey Keenan. It's good to see you again."

It really was good to see him. Tonight he had on a short-sleeve button down shirt with his signature jeans. His dreads were loose coils falling to his shoulders. I could never tire of looking at him. He sat down beside me and ordered a drink for himself and a second one for me. Suddenly it dawned on me that I hadn't seen Kyle. Not surprisingly, Keenan informed me that Kyle had gotten caught up with some female before he even reached VIP.

"You've got to be kidding me", I exclaimed in disbelief. "That boy is something else." Keenan smirked, "Yeah, he is…but what's a man to do when there are so many beautiful women in Atlanta. I thought that whole Georgia peaches thing was a myth."

I studied his profile, wondering how many women he had been with since arriving in Atlanta. It wouldn't surprise me if he was a player. Kyle was his cousin after all and he looked too good for women not to be throwing themselves at him. Tonight, my mind had been set…I planned on hooking up with him, but I wanted to know what I was getting myself into before I became too involved.

We spent more time conversing before Dawn and Kyle unceremoniously interrupted our flow. There were hugs and kisses all around as Dawn greeted Keenan like an old friend. I questioned Dawn about "Stalker" but she just smiled in that slick way of hers and told me that she was meeting up with him after the club. Typical Dawn.

"So Kyle," I spoke, turning to address him, "I see you're making up for the lost time that you were in D.C."

"Awww girl, stop being so jealous. You know I will always have plenty of love left for you."

"Whatever… just keep your little chicken heads under control because Dawn and I didn't come here tonight to fight." Right on cue, Dawn chimed in, "Damn right, I came here to get my groove on." With that, she grabbed Kyle's hand and headed to the main dance floor downstairs.

I walked over to the balcony attempting to get a better view of the crowd. More people in the lounge started dancing as the DJ started playing all of the latest hot tracks back to back. The effects of my second drink started to have an impact on my senses. Solo, I started dancing by the rail. I was lost in my own mental groove when I felt hands on my waist. This time I knew exactly who those hands belonged to.

I never stopped moving. Instead, I put my hands on his as we started rocking together in a perfect, synchronized, rhythm. I leaned back against his strong chest, feeling the whisper of his breath on my neck. His arms encircled my waist as I continued to grind against him. I was so turned on, but I could tell that I wasn't the only one. The evidence of his own arousal was prominent, which pleased me tremendously. This was all the confirmation that I needed that the chemistry between us was definitely real. I turned around to face him, putting my arms around his neck. I stared into his eyes and saw the lust that he couldn't conceal. I allowed him to see mine. Our bodies were sweaty from the heat of the club and our own growing passion. He broke the spell by calling my name.

"Toni…I want to kiss you, can I kiss you?" I didn't answer him. I couldn't. I just nodded yes, pulling his head towards me, meeting him halfway. Our eyes continued to be locked in as his soft lips brushed mine. The initial gentleness gave way to raw desire as he parted my lips with his tongue allowing me to taste him. I wrapped his dreads around my hands and pulled him in deeper. His mouth was wet and hot and I found myself moaning in response.

We were so engrossed in each other that neither of us noticed that Dawn and Kyle had come back upstairs until I heard Dawn's voice, "Well, well."

I instantly pulled away from Keenan, slightly embarrassed by our public display. I noticed that other people in the lounge were also staring. I couldn't say anything because I was still light-headed from a combination of the kiss and the alcohol. Kyle was standing behind her with a shocked expression on his face.

When he finally spoke, a hint of anger could be detected in his voice, "Damn, what kind of conversation took place while we were gone?"

It was evident from the look on his face that he was not pleased with me nor Keenan. In fact, he barely looked in my direction, choosing instead to stare at Keenan as if he wanted to physically assault him. Keenan stared back. I nervously laughed, trying to break the tension that I could I sense increasing by the minute.

"Hey...you know me...alcohol and music."

Dawn, not one to take any situation too seriously, smugly stated, "Girl please, you don't have to answer to us. You two are grown so handle your business. I'm about to get out of here though because you know I'm meeting Craig."

Back to reality.

"Who the hell is Craig?"

"Craig aka Stalker, Toni, you know I told you I was meeting him after the club."

"Yeah, I'm sorry...I do remember." I announced that I was also leaving. I then looked around at Kyle and Keenan. I realized that as much as I loved Kyle, I was not willing to let this opportunity with Keenan pass, especially now that he and I had made a connection. I briefly glanced at Kyle, before reaching out to grab Keenan's hand. He looked at me and I could see the questions hovering in his eyes. I answered by bluntly asking him if he was coming home with me. He responded with that smile I had already come to love.

Kyle, who was still sulking stated, "Keenan, I know you're grown, but Toni is like my sister. You need to be really careful about how you're going to handle this situation."

Keenan replied, "Trust me, Kyle, I would not hurt Toni…besides, I don't think we even have a situation yet."

Dawn interrupted the verbal duel by stating that we should all call it a night and discuss this "situation" at a later date. We followed her outside of the club then headed to our respective cars. After promising Dawn that I would call her tomorrow, I gave Kyle a hug, mentally noting his stiff response. Undaunted, me and Keenan rushed to my car, disturbed about Kyle's response, yet excited about tonight's possibilities

....

The ride to my house was brief, yet tense. A ball of nervous energy, I made unnecessary adjustments to my seat, the radio, the mirror, anything to keep my mind off of the situation before me. I kept glancing at Keenan in the passenger seat. We hadn't spoken since we entered the car. I reached over and rubbed my hand along his muscular thigh, feeling the tension even through his jeans. He gazed at me, eyes smoldering, and wrapped my hand in his. Heat radiated from his fingertips. I wanted this man so badly.

Once we arrived, I hesitated for a moment in an attempt to calm my nerves, all the while questioning if this was what I really wanted. I knew without a doubt that once I allowed this man to enter my home, I would also be allowing him to enter my heart, a possession I had carefully guarded over the last couple of years. It was too soon to determine if he was worth the risk. My only considerations would be the undeniable and magnetic chemistry between us. After doing a quick mental pros and con list, I decided our chemistry alone would make it a risk I was willing to take.

After unlocking the door, I turned off the alarm, quickly resetting it after Keenan entered behind me. I turned to him with the intention of asking if he wanted something to drink…instead he grabbed my hands and pulled me into an embrace. I melted into his warmth, wrapping my arms around his waist.

Once more I found myself immersed in his scent…the smell of him, dizzying. He grasped my waist and with his fingers began tracing small circles on my lower back. I gasped in response as he started to kiss my neck, the heat and wetness leaving a lingering trail to my waiting, parted mouth. Moans escaped the walls of my throat when his tongue finally discovered my own. Deliberately, I ran my fingers from his waist to his chest and up to his beautiful face. I allowed them to remain for a moment, enjoying the velvet texture of his skin. All the while, his tongue continued to assault my mouth. We both moaned as our desires escalated. His hands journeyed from my waist to my breasts. He massaged my soft flesh through the thin material of my shirt…using his thumbs to slightly graze my nipples, which instantly hardened in reaction to his touch. He finally pulled away from my mouth, using his hot tongue to replace his hands on my breasts. I moaned louder as he started to gently suck my nipples…screamed when I felt the repetitious circles of his tongue.

The reins of control were slipping beyond my grasp. Suddenly, consumed with indescribable fear, I pulled his mouth away and lifted his head. I read the desire in his eyes, but I forced myself to look away. Slowly, I disengaged from his embrace. I tried to catch my breath…a difficult task considering that my body was still tingling and aching.

"Keenan…I'm so sorry. I just…I just need to think for a minute."

He sighed, nervously running his hands across his face.

"No Toni, I'm the one who's sorry. I really did not mean to move that fast with you. I just…damn girl…I have just been thinking about you since the first day I saw you."=

We both laughed aloud at the clichéd statement. My thoughts were spinning as I tried to figure out how much of my feelings to disclose. For some reason, my heart advised me to be true, even though my mind screamed caution.

I walked to the sofa and slowly sank into it. Keenan walked over to the chaise, kicked off his Timberlands, and settled into his now familiar position. I gazed at his outstretched legs… let my eyes wander up to his face. Allowing my heart to guide my words, I expressed my attraction to him. Nevertheless, I also expressed my fear…how afraid I was of moving too fast for fear of losing my mind and my heart. Silently, I watched, as he digested my words. Still…motionless. Eventually he responded, "Toni, I'm going to be honest with you, I am so incredibly attracted to you. But, I'm not going to lie to you. I'm just getting out of a long-term relationship so if a relationship or any type of commitment is what you're looking for, I'm not that guy." I wondered whether or not the relationship he mentioned was a part of the fresh start he previously spoke of at the store.

His confession failed to unnerve me. I was not in a desperate state to find a man. My career was my life and besides, I was never the woman who felt as if I needed to have a man in order to feel complete. But, I was tired of spending too many nights alone. After assessing the situation, I concluded that Keenan could add some much needed spice to my life. I made the decision to accept what I believed he was offering…friendship, companionship, intimacy.

Temporarily comforted by our conversation, I rose from the sofa, walked to the chaise, and reached out to him. He hesitated momentarily before taking my hand…asking if I was sure I could handle what he was willing to give. I reassured him by leaning in and kissing him softly.

Slowly…the tension released from his body as I began to gently tug then nibble on his bottom lip. He stood up, never removing his mouth from mine. As he began to unbutton my shirt, my nipples again hardened in anticipation of his touch. There was no sense of urgency in his movements; it was as if he, as well as I, was trying to savor each kiss, touch…taste.

We parted only long enough to remove the remainder of our clothing. When the entirety of his body was revealed, I stood in awe. He was one beautiful man. His brown skin glowed with a mist of perspiration. His thighs were toned, his chest defined, his waist narrow. He reached for me. This time there was only a raw hunger between us as we explored each other's bodies. His fingers found the source of my heat and stroked me unceasingly to the brink of explosion. He ravaged my breasts with his mouth, sucking then biting my nipples until I cried out in a fusion of pleasure and pain. I grasped his now enlarged manhood, begging him to take me. He flipped me on my back, sliding my body to the edge of the chaise. He was on his knees, waiting, watching me squirm, moan, beg, all without saying a word. Suddenly, I felt his swollen manhood at the entrance. I needed him. When he finally entered me I almost had an instant orgasm. He filled me completely, perfectly. I screamed his name as he moaned mine, our bodies dancing to an almost natural cadence. I entwined my arms around his waist as our motions quickened. My body reacted to his own stroke for stroke until…simultaneously we climaxed…crying out to each other…clinging to each other as our passions exploded.

       ....

It was a few minutes before either of us moved or spoke. We lay with our bodies entangled, waiting for our breaths to return to their normal rhythms. I was afraid to move…fearful of fracturing the moment. It should have been easy. As a young, single woman, sex was definitely not taboo; however, the moment Keenan took possession of my body, I knew that this relationship was going to be different from any other I had experienced. It wasn't just the sex, which proved to be incredible, it was more of the emotions I felt when I first met him…that immense, soulful connection. Keenan shifted above me, rising up on one elbow. He grinned at me, with that beautiful smile.

"Ms. Toni…that was unbelievable girl."

"Oh yeah? Well you weren't too bad yourself Mr. Jackson."

He just laughed as he rolled over on his back. I got up off of the lounge; we were barely fitting on it together anyway, and walked into the kitchen. The clock on the wall noted that it was 3:30 a.m. I grabbed two bottles of water out of the refrigerator, gave one to Keenan and walked over to my original place on the sofa. I found the remote to the CD player and turned it on, releasing the soulful sounds of Anthony Hamilton who was professing his undying love to "Charlene."

Under normal circumstances I would have had an exit plan in place to get a guy out of my house, but these were no ordinary circumstances. I did not want Keenan to leave, but I did not know how to ask him to stay. With our prior conversation still ringing in my ears…I didn't want to come off as needy or clingy. My pride would not allow it.

He finally sat up, his actions being the exact opposite of what I expected, or wanted. He gathered his clothes and began to dress. Once he was finished, he walked over to the sofa and pulled me to my feet. I didn't resist as he pulled me into an embrace and kissed me tenderly on the forehead.

"I have to go." *Please stay.*

"I understand." *I need you.*

I walked over to the phone and called a cab. I walked back to Keenan and silently wrapped my arms around his neck. I just needed him to hold me, no words necessary. He must have sensed my mood because he lightly kissed my forehead, my face, avoiding my lips. I lay my head on his shoulder while he rocked me and stroked my hair. We remained that way until the spell was broken by the horn from the cab. Words still unspoken, I regretfully pulled away from him, grabbed his hand, and slowly walked him to the door. He kissed my forehead one last time before walking outside. I stood for a moment feeling a strange sense of loneliness. How could it be that I was already missing him? I turned off the CD player, switched off the lights and went to bed wondering how much trouble this man would prove to be.

Chapter 5: Dilemma

I must be losing my damn mind. I can't believe that I just had sex with Toni. Kyle is going to kill me once he finds out and there is no doubt in my mind that he will find out. The question is, does he need to hear it from me or should I let Toni handle it. Or maybe he doesn't have to find out at all. I mean, it's not like I plan on sleeping with her again. Hell, I never planned on sleeping with her in the first place. I don't know what it is but I really meant it when I said I had been thinking about her since the first night I spent hanging out at her house. I should have had my guard up. I should have been prepared. I mean…Kyle has always talked about her. About how beautiful she is…body and spirit. Still, I was unprepared for the natural, earthly beauty she was in person. That shock of naturally curly hair. That smooth cocoa skin. Those deep brown eyes…that smile…and that damn body. She was my idea of perfection. Yeah…I definitely knew I was in trouble when I met her.

I should have stayed my ass in D.C. Maybe then I wouldn't have found myself in this predicament. Instead, here I am, in Atlanta surrounded by temptation every day with a variety of attractive women. Moving to Atlanta has proven to be a blessing and a curse. Kyle was absolutely right. It is a great place to get a new lease on life…to breathe again. The city is an artist's haven. One of the few wise decisions I made in my life was to leave the corporate world and to follow my heart. Since I've been here, I've been painting and writing as if my soul has been starved. Every day it's been a new journey of awakenings. For the first time in a long time I feel free.

But I'm not free. Not yet anyway. Which is why I've been so careful not to get too involved with anyone since I've been here. Then…I meet Toni and now my mind's all fucked up. Why the hell didn't I leave the club with Kyle? He tried to give me an out, but like most men, I let my dick guide me instead of my brain. I know that I can't sleep with her again. I need to file her away as just another meaningless hook-up. The problem is…all week long all I've thought about is her. *Damn.* Her sex was good. I can still smell her…and feel the smoothness of her skin on my fingertips. I can still taste her.

I called her once…just to hear the sound of her voice. To be respectful at least, I should have called her the next day, however, that would have been against my personal rule. Instead, I took the coward's way out by calling her at a time when I knew that she would be at the store. Our conversation was fleeting, but I promised to call her again soon. I'm not even sure I plan on keeping that promise. Honestly, for both of our sakes I shouldn't.

Or maybe I should. I mean Toni is a grown woman. I told her that I wasn't ready for anything serious before she even decided to sleep with me. She's a beautiful woman… why shouldn't I allow myself to get to know her better. As long as we keep everything in perspective it should all be good.

But what the hell should I do about Kyle. *Damn.*

This train of thought was leading me nowhere. I decided to go for a run in order to clear my head. Hastily, I pulled on my sweats and sneakers, grabbed my iPod, and headed out the door. My small apartment is in an area of Atlanta named Little Five Points. It's known for its diverse and "artsy" crowd. Freedom Park is nearby so I headed that way, eager to take my mind away from this madness.

After running for about forty-five minutes, I began the journey back to my apartment. I had worked up a sweat, so I decided to take a shower. The water felt exhilarating as it rained over my head and body. I hoped that the shower would help to wash away the thoughts of Toni consuming my mind, but that wasn't proving to be the case. Closing my eyes, I gave in to the memories of her kiss and the feel of her skin. Her wild abandon at lovemaking that perfectly matched my own uninhibited, free style. Noting my body's response, I could not deny that I missed her, which was definitely a problem. Frustrated, I turned off the water, shook the excess water from my dreadlocks, and wrapped a towel around my waist. As I stepped out of the shower, my cell phone started ringing. Instantly, I recognized the number. *Damn.*

"Keenan." I answered, making no attempt to mask my irritation.

"Wow, you answered your phone. I can't believe it" was the sarcastic reply on the other end.

"Please don't start Sarai. What do you want?"

"What do you mean what do I want? Do I have to have an excuse to call my *husband* now? Is that the way it is between us?"

Damn I thought, running my hands across my face...this was not the conversation I wanted to be having.

"Sarai, stop being so dramatic and tell me what you want. I have a lot going on today."

My wife, the mother of my child, breathed heavily on the other end of the phone. I wanted to give her the benefit of the doubt...this separation had not been easy for either of us, but I was not willing to go there with her...not today.

When she answered, her tone of voice had changed...it was softer...as if she didn't want to have this fight either.

"Look Keenan, I'm sorry. I just...I had a really tough week at the office and I needed to talk to you. I needed my *husband*."

I hate it when she does this to me. When she corners me in this difficult place where there are no easy answers.

Yes, I am a married man. Sort of. Sarai and I have been separated for months. Our story is really no different than any other couple going through what is generally considered a rough patch. We love each other, but somewhere along this journey we lost sight of each other. Both of us have chosen career paths that have led us in completely different directions. Sarai is very business-minded, something I initially loved about her. She's very ambitious, very smart, and very talented. *However*...her ambition has become stronger than her need to keep us close...me close. When I made the decision to leave my job at the marketing firm, she was not only angry, she was resentful. We stopped communicating, we stopped *loving*.

There is a bond between us that will never be broken. That bond is my five year old daughter Zy'riah, the true love of my life. The main reason why I am separated, and not officially divorced.

Leaving D.C, leaving Zy'riah, was the hardest decision that I've ever had to make in my life. Yet, it was one I had to make. I knew that as long as I stayed in the same area as Sarai, I would never be able to think clearly, to clear the fog that had become an ever present companion in my head...to get a clear indication on what I needed to do about our relationship. So, when Kyle offered me a lifeline, I graciously accepted.

The silence between us on the phone was a clear representative of the chasm that had developed in our relationship.

"Sarai, I can't do this right now. I can't be your husband when it's a matter of convenience. That's not the way we decided to play this so please respect this space that *we* decided *we* needed."

Again, silence.

"You know what Keenan, just forget I called. I don't know why I even call you because you act like we're already over, when we're supposed to be figuring things out. I didn't decide to quit us. I only agreed to space."

I could hear her voice getting thick with emotion. This situation was quickly going from bad to worse.

I sighed again. "Ok Sarai, for this moment I am here." So I let her vent, I let her cry, and then, as was becoming all too common, I let her go.

I wanted to speak to Zy'riah before Sarai got off of the phone, but I didn't want to extend the conversation any more than necessary. I hate these conversations with Sarai. They always leave me feeling like an utter failure, as a husband and as a father.

As the calming effects of the shower disintegrated I realized that I needed an escape. I needed Toni.

Chapter 6: Choosing

I must be losing my damn mind. I can't believe I'm going this crazy about a man. All week long I've found myself constantly thinking about Keenan and I didn't like it at all. This was so unlike me. Once a man has left the bedroom, he's gone from all thoughts unless he was good enough for my mind to conjure up on some random, horny night. This wasn't proving to be the case with Keenan. I found myself not only thinking about him, but physically longing for him...aching to feel him inside of me, to feel his skin, to taste his kiss.

Luckily, my days were filled with the everyday business of the store; however, my nights were an altogether different story. Over the past week, I had developed a routine of putting on some smooth music, grabbing a glass of wine, getting in a quick shower... suffering the nights alone. I could have called an old friend to dull my ache, but I only wanted Keenan.

The problem is...I'm not sure how much of me he actually wants. I only heard from him once this week. Even then, I couldn't talk to him for any extended time. I guess I could have called him, but I didn't want to seem like some school girl with her first crush. So I found myself waiting by the phone for him to call. He only called that once though, now I'm just...confused. I thought it was a little bit more than a one night stand, but maybe I was wrong. Maybe to him, that's all it was. For the first time in a long time, I felt vulnerable. That old insecurity was rearing its ugly head. This was too much.

....

I was on my way to Dawn and Rae's house to pick up Lexie. Mia had been hired as an official employee of Muse so I called her in and gave myself a much needed day off. Unfortunately, as soon as Dawn found out, she reeled me into babysitting for a few hours while she went on a date with Stalker aka Craig. Jamie had been scheduled to spend the day with her, but, once again, he was a no-show, Rather than hear about the drama all morning, I pulled myself out of bed, drove across town, and was now about to ring the doorbell.

Rae answered the door and the smile and hug I gave her were more than genuine. I had not seen my friend in over a week. I hadn't even talked to her to give her an update on what had transpired between me and Keenan. My life had been just that hectic. She hugged me back before letting me in. The aroma of hazelnut coffee greeted me. Following the scent, I headed straight to the kitchen to get my first cup of the day.

"I swear girl, I don't see how you can work in a coffee shop all day and still have a craving."

I laughed, locating my special cup that I keep here for these occasions.

"Rae, you know coffee is my source of life. Besides, I would have stopped by Starbuck's if Dawn wasn't panicking like it was an emergency. Anyway...if you're here, please explain to me why she needed me."

Rae got the creamer out of the refrigerator before answering.

"I can't do it. I signed up for a writing workshop at Emory. For months I've been procrastinating about it but I finally decided to pay the money and do it. I should be finished around five though so I will call you to see what's up for tonight...*that's* if you don't still have Lexie."

She was absolutely right about that. Knowing Dawn, a few hours could very well turn into the whole night if things went as planned with Craig.

No sooner had the thought flashed across my mind when Dawn came flying around the corner, almost knocking Rae over.. "Damn girlfriend, where is the fire?" I joked with her. Dawn apologized to Rae before looking up at me with fire in her eyes.

"Do not start with me. Craig will be here any minute, but I'm running late having to deal with Jamie. I have been on the phone cursing him out for standing Lexie up again today. I just don't get it. I'm beginning to wonder if he hates me so much that he would purposely hurt our daughter just to spite me."

I took a sip of my coffee while I thought about Dawn's predicament. I would be just as frustrated if I were in her shoes. Lexie worshiped the ground that Jamie walked on, and because of this, Dawn would often cover for him when he didn't show up as he promised. The last thing she wanted was for Lexie to question Jamie's love, but she was getting tired of him always leaving her to clean up his mess.

Rae tried to calm Dawn's nerves. "Girl get yourself together and don't allow Jamie to ruin your day, which was possibly his plan all along."

I agreed, "Come on Dawn, I've got big plans for me and Lexie today, so just have fun and don't even sweat Jamie's sorry ass."

She paused before taking a deep breath. "You know what, you ladies are so right, as usual. Forget Jamie, I'm about to have a great day with a *real* man."

"Oh yeah," I stated, raising an eyebrow. "You've got to tell me how you ended up going on a date with Craig the Stalker."

Dawn started laughing and told me how she called Craig one night when Lexie was with her cousin. Until then, their only interactions had been at various clubs and one really early breakfast. He seemed really cool, so when he asked her out on a real date, she accepted. At first, she hesitated. She was not trying to get too serious with anyone, especially since she and Jamie had only been divorced for six months. At this point in her life she was just about having fun and taking care of her daughter.

That night she and Craig ended up hanging out this trendy sports bar named Legend's in downtown Atlanta. She was curious as to how he would act outside of the club atmosphere, but she was pleasantly surprised that he was a gentleman the entire night. They left Legend's and walked around Centennial Park simply talking and enjoying each other's company. She found herself wanting to invite him back to her house, but cautioned herself not to move too quickly...fearing that she could put herself in the category of a one-night stand.

As she spoke, I thought about Keenan. Perhaps he wasn't calling because we had sex too soon. By sleeping with him, did I put myself in that unwarranted booty call category? That would have been okay, if I hadn't felt the connection between us. I wondered if I would get the opportunity to undo the damage that had been done.

I tuned back in to Dawn just as she was mentioning that Craig was taking her to breakfast and then to the Aquarium.

"Well, let me go make sure my little Lexie has some extra clothes because the way your date is sounding, she may not get picked up until Sunday night."

We all laughed just as we heard a car outside of the house. Dawn peeked out of the window then walked over to open the door. If this was Craig walking towards the house, then he was even finer than I remembered him. He was tall, dark, and lean, but definitely not skinny, which was my perception at the club. He was dressed casually in a pair of jeans and a t-shirt and was rocking aviator shades. As he got closer, he took the shades off and blessed Dawn with a striking smile.

"Good morning beautiful," he spoke in a wonderfully rich voice.

Dawn answered with a Hollywood worthy smile of her own. I glanced at Rae who seemed to be in as much awe and admiration of Craig as I was. Dawn, as if finally remembering that Rae and I were even in the room, turned to us with introductions.

"Craig, these are my best friends, Rayna, Rae, and Toni. You probably remember Toni from Visions."

Craig greeted both of us casually, but he instantly diverted his attention back to Dawn. He asked if she was ready to go, and when she replied yes, he took her hand and led her out to his car, an older model silver Audi. After watching Dawn leave, Rae did an exaggerated swipe of sweat from her forehead and leaned against the door.

"Lawd that was one fine specimen of a man."

I laughed at her crazy self. "Girl get your silly self out of this house before you end up late to your workshop. Let me go wake up my baby so we can get going."

I left Rae swooning in the doorway and made my way to Lexie's room. As I walked through her door, a sense of tranquility enclosed me. Dawn has done an excellent job of decorating her room. The minute you opened her door, it felt like walking into the story book version of heaven. There were clouds and stars painted all over the ceiling and walls. Bible verses were inscribed along the borders. Her bed was queen sized, even though she was only five, complete with numerous pillows and stuffed animals. I walked over to the bed, locating her tiny frame among the covers.

Even sleeping, she was gorgeous, just like mom. Lexie is a child who lights up a room whenever she is around. Dawn always jokes that she will be her ticket out of the hood. Never does she miss an opportunity to perform whenever she senses that she has a willing audience. And her performances never fail to disappoint. At five, she never ceases to amaze me with her uncanny ability to watch videos of popular artists and mimic their movements. At the moment, she was laying on her side, snoring lightly. Her long, black hair, inherited from Dawn, framed her small face. Her thick eyebrows and caramel skin were traits that were both inherited from her father.

I hated to wake her, but I needed to get back to my house soon to get some work done. I leaned over her and nudged her neck with my nose, inhaling her sweet child-like scent. At times like this, I wonder what it would be like to have a child of my own, to have a little person in the world who looks like me, laughs like me, and has my smile or my personality. Just as swiftly as the thought appeared, it vanished. I was a long way from having a child. Lord knows, I hadn't even fulfilled the prerequisite of finding a man.

Lexie stirred slightly. I ruffled her hair and tickled her nose until she was fully awake. The moment she recognized me she jumped into my arms.

"Auntie Toni," she exclaimed. "What are you here for?"

"Hi baby. I came to pick you up so you can spend the entire day with me. Mommy is going to be busy today."

For a minute it appeared that she would sulk. In her child-like pout, she told me that Dawn had promised her pancakes. I wasn't sure if that was an actual promise or whether or not this was Lexie's way of manipulating me. Anyway, I agreed to take her to IHOP before we headed to my house. After making sure I would stand by my promise, she jumped out of bed and went to the bathroom to brush her teeth. When she finished, I pulled her long hair into a ponytail and packed her an overnight bag. She quickly dressed. By now it was almost 10 a.m. and my stomach was alerting me that I was also starving. On the way out of the door, I grabbed Lexie's booster seat, got her strapped in and we headed to IHOP to get our grub on.

....

As expected, Lexie ended up sleeping over. I really wanted to hate Dawn for being so lucky but it was impossible to do. At least one of us was getting some love.

It was one of those rare Sunday mornings when I had absolutely nothing on my agenda. I slept in...utterly exhausted from dealing with Lexie yesterday. Not only did we have breakfast, but somehow she coaxed me into taking her to the Children's Museum. The museum has interactive displays and stations and Lexie being the little tornado that she is, wanted to touch every single one. I, the designated playmate, felt obligated to crawl, pull, jump, and touch as much as she did. At least all of the playing served its purpose. Lexie was asleep before 8 o'clock and I had the rest of the night to enjoy by myself. Unfortunately, I was exactly that...by myself.

I called Dawn to see if she had made it home, but there was no answer. Luckily, Rae answered her phone on the first ring. She agreed to keep Lexie for me until Dawn made it back to the house. When Lexie finished eating her oatmeal, we loaded up the car and headed back down 85.

Approaching the house, my level of excitement rose. It had been too long since Rae and I had free time sit and catch up with each other's lives. With me being at the cafe and her new position often demanding her to work overtime, our conversations have dwindled to five minute sessions of words. Today seemed like the perfect day to have coffee and update her on everything, or rather, lack of anything that had occurred between me and Keenan.

I walked up the narrow driveway and rang the doorbell. Rae answered within seconds, already anticipating our arrival. Lexie and I both gave her quick hugs before Lexie charged through the room and out of the sliding glass door which served as the gateway to her world. Anyone visiting the home would think that more than one child lived at the residence with the numerous toys sprawled around the small, enclosed space of a yard.

Before I could call out to her to put away her overnight bag, she was already out of the door. I put the bag in a corner and settled on the only oversized recliner in the room, my favorite spot. When I moved into my house, I allowed Rae to keep the furniture we once shared. I wanted to ensure that my first home was decorated in my own signature style. There was a moment, after Dawn moved in, that Rae thought about changing it; however, after witnessing a five-year old's endless adventures of spilled drinks, food stains, and minor collisions, she wisely decided that it would be a waste of money to invest in anything new. I watched and waited while Rae put on a pot of coffee, then returned, sitting opposite of me on the sofa.

"So," she prodded, her eyes betraying her eagerness.

I began telling her about how things escalated between me and Keenan at the club, before providing her the intimate details of our incredible lovemaking session. I'm not the type of girl to "kiss and tell", but Rae is my best friend and having been through a lot together from our college days until now, there wasn't much about our lives that was off limits.

"Rae, I'm not sure what that man has done to me, I can't stop thinking about him." I exclaimed, once I completed the accounts of the night.

Silence. I already knew what she was thinking. The same thing I have been thinking in these days since that night. How the hell did I fall so quickly? This was definitely not my style. Ever since the Greg fiasco, I have managed to keep my heart guarded and my mind focused. As a single woman in Atlanta, I do have opportunities, even with the seemingly dominant population of gay black men, but there have been no serious emotions involved. Now here I was acting like a fool over some black Adonis I barely knew.

"Wow Toni, is this really happening to *you?*" She joked.

"Shut up, I can't believe it either. You know I have never let any dick get me riled up like this, but girl I'm telling you there is something about this man that speaks to me and my entire body just responds with no thought. I don't know about this Rae. I don't like this feeling of being out of control."

Rae stopped laughing and was looking at me with a genuine look of disbelief registered on her face. Because she was my best friend, she would be. I'm sure she, just as I did, expected Keenan to be another fling. Someone for me to enjoy and have fun with until the initial excitement inevitably ran its course. This felt different.

"Look Toni, I think that you are making too much out of this. I mean yeah I am surprised that you are willing to tear down your wall of emotions so soon, but let's be honest, you have been working hard for years so it's time for you to have something real. You deserve it. Just proceed with caution and promise me you won't let Kyle interfere. Let me know if you need for me to fight that battle for you."

Undoubtedly, she would. During our college years, I considered myself lucky to have two best friends who were extremely protective of me. Because of Rae's own history with men, she was like a pint-sized pit bull when it came to me dating. She was tough, a product of Atlanta's streets and having grown up the only girl among boys. If she sensed that any of my relationships were becoming remotely serious, she transformed into Colombo.

On the other hand, Kyle was more like an overbearing big brother. At one point it seemed as if his life purpose was keeping tabs on who I was dating. Although mutual friends believed his protectiveness stemmed from jealousy, I knew he was genuinely concerned. I could only imagine the drama that was sure to unfold if he found out that I had actually slept with Keenan. Although I regretted the circumstances, I didn't regret it enough to stop seeing Keenan. Then again, I reminded myself, it all may be a moot point because Keenan may have stopped seeing me without notice.

I remained at Rae's for a few more hours before leaving to go back to the house. As I was driving, I thought about Keenan and the fact that he had not called. Usually, I am not the type of female to chase a man, but I just couldn't understand why he hadn't called me when the night we shared was so amazing, or so I thought. I decided to take a chance and give him a call, promising myself that if I didn't reach him, I would not call back…that I would wait for him to reach out to me, if he ever did.

The phone rang several times before he answered. I paused for a minute, thrilled to hear his voice. Anxious now that he was actually on the phone.

"Hey Keenan, it's Toni." I heard him pause on the line, but I couldn't translate the meaning of it. Was he busy? Did he not want to hear from me?

"What's up Toni? It's *really* good to hear from you." I smiled even though he could not see my face. *Exhale.*

Almost immediately, Keenan began apologizing for not calling me. He said he had been busy trying to get some of his furniture and other items transported from D.C to Atlanta. *Ok.* Recognizing his statement for the excuse that it was, I let it slide. I told him that I had been busy as well and gave him a brief rundown of some of the events that had been going on at Muse. Sensing an opening, I conveyed to him how happy I was to have the day off. Then taking a leap of faith, I asked him if he would like to share the rest of the day with me. This time there was no hesitation when he replied, "yes."

Chapter 7: Stop This Train

Here I go again. Somehow, I can't seem to get off of this train of self-destruction. It seemed that my desire for Toni had intensified ever since my conversation with Sarai, but so far I had done a good job of not acting on my thoughts. Until today. Until she called and I heard her sexy voice on the phone calling me into her world...again. Yet again I couldn't resist. I knew that I should. I was supposed to, but I didn't...I couldn't. In one breath of a moment I decided that I didn't want to avoid this woman anymore...I wanted to be let in. So here I was...waiting for her to arrive at my apartment...excited...nervous...like a hormonal, teen aged boy. Crazy.

I lit some candles and turned on some music...Brian McKnight seemed perfect for the occasion. Thirty minutes later the doorbell rang and I answered, inviting her into my space. *Damn.* She's so beautiful. I could have kicked myself for not calling her sooner.

"Hey you." was my greeting. She smiled a smile that I'm sure has broken many hearts...

"Hey back." was her response. As she walked in I made mental notes of her appearance. Even dressed casually in a pair of blue Victoria Secrets sweatpants and a thin cotton t-shirt, she was the definition of sexy. The sweatpants hugged her ass perfectly. Her hair was pulled in her usual ponytail, but this time it was positioned in a loose ball on the top of her head. She wore no make-up, only lip gloss on her full lips. If you didn't know the truth, you would think she was only in her early twenties, rather than her early thirties.

I must have been staring because she began to nervously play with her hair and started apologizing for not going home to change first. I reassured her that she was just fine the way she was. Not being able to resist any longer, I deliberately walked over to her and pulled her into an embrace. The scent of vanilla engulfed me. She wrapped her arms around my waist and we just stood in the middle of the floor holding each other.

Damn. I knew at that moment that all of my reservations were out of the window. I wanted to know this girl, right or wrong. And the fall-out that was destined to come…well I would just suffer the consequences. For now, I just wanted to be in this moment…no thoughts of Kyle, Sarai, or even Zy'riah. Just me and this brown-skinned beauty that had me wrapped in her embrace.

After what seemed like forever, we finally pulled away. I kissed her on the forehead, then stole a small kiss on her lips. They were slightly sweet from the flavored lip gloss she was wearing.

"So…you missed me?" I joked, trying to break the hint of tension that was still in the air.

She laughed. "Maybe…a little bit."

I directed her towards the sofa.

"I see you got your furniture", she observed, looking around my small apartment. In the weeks since I last saw her, I finally got the furniture and some other items that I had in storage in D.C. Even with the furniture, my apartment was a work in progress. I am not the one for decorating. Sarai took charge of decorating our home. My only contribution in that area were my original pieces strategically hung in various areas of the house. Still, with its muted gray tones and soft light, the apartment was cozy.

She walked to the couch, finding a comfortable place to lounge. She was looking so sexy leaning back, that I wanted nothing more than to undress her right then and there. However, I was hesitant to make that kind of a bold move. Although she had made the first step by coming over, I wasn't quite sure where we stood or what she wanted. I'm sure she had many questions as to why I hadn't called or tried to contact her.

As if reading my thoughts, she quickly turned to me when I sat down beside her.

"So, Mr. Jackson, where do you think we are going with *this*?" Her dark brown eyes were full of questions that I did not have the answers to. I should have been prepared to have this conversation, but I wasn't.

In the moment that Toni entered my space today I could no longer deny my attraction to her. But, there was another world in which I existed, one in which I was a father and a husband. I couldn't envision the two worlds co-existing, yet the selfish part of me could not see letting this woman walk away without examining all of our possibilities. Crazy…I walked away from DC to find peace and now I've found myself hovering on the edge of chaos.

I jumped.

"I want you." I heard the words coming from my mouth but I was powerless to stop them. Once the flood-gate was open, they poured like wine from my tongue.

I turned to face her so that she could easily read my emotions.

"Toni, I want you. I want to be with you, to get to know everything about you. Let's just take *this,* whatever it becomes, one day…hour…minute at a time. That's what I can give right now." There was a brief moment of silence before she finally spoke. *What did she want from me?* If she wanted more…needed more, I would have to walk away.

"Ok." I finally heard her speak. "Ok…let's do *this.*" She gave a slight chuckle then sighed before reaching up to touch my face.

I turned and kissed the palm of her hand… planted soft kisses on her fingers and wrist. She sharply inhaled.

Her vanilla flavor left traces of sweetness on my tongue. I could feel my body responding. I felt her free hand in my hair, slowly twisting. Then… her fingers lightly traced the side of my face and neck. I closed my eyes, losing myself in her butterfly touches. I inhaled the sweet scent of her breath before I felt the softness of her lips on mine. Slowly I sucked in her full lips. I needed to taste her.

We both moaned as our passion heightened. I didn't want to pull away but our clothes were unwelcomed barriers, preventing me from touching more of her silky skin. Hurriedly, we undressed. As we found ourselves naked in front of each other yet again, I was amazed at how beautiful she was. Her skin glowed and although she was petite in frame, her hips were perfectly rounded…thighs thick, just like the brothers like them. Her breasts were small, but full. Her dark brown nipples, already erect from her excitement, were a perfect contrast against her smooth brown skin. They invited me to kiss them.

We came together like magnetic forces drawn together. As I wrapped my arms around her small waist, we fell to the sofa with her on top. Kissing, touching, tasting, breathing…we created our own orchestra of sounds.

"Toni, Toni," I spoke her name over and over, lost in the moment.

"Yes baby," she breathlessly responded…"tell me what you need, tell me what you want me to do."

I looked into her eyes that were now dark with passion. "Love me." I answered.

There were no other words between us as she took me…all of me…into all of her. Her wetness and warmth embraced me…the slow movements of her body rocked me. I thought I would lose my mind. As she leaned in closer I could feel her breath on my ear accompanied by her soft moans. I grabbed her waist as our dance began. Gently we rocked, her womanhood gripping me with every thrust. Her soft moans got louder as our thrusts got quicker.

I was trying my best to hold on but all of a sudden she grabbed my hair and screamed, "Ah Keenan, baby, please cum with me…cum with me." Her sensual hips rolled against me and I lost all control. All of the passion that was pent up inside of my body suddenly erupted within her.

....

Unlike our last time together we lay for what seemed like forever. Toni had collapsed on top of me and hadn't yet moved. I was stroked her back, ran my fingers through the soft curls of her ponytail. All the while Maxwell, who had now replaced Brian McKnight on the CD player, was fittingly singing "whenever, wherever, whatever."

Many thoughts clouded the space in my head. Feeling her body against me was much too comfortable. She didn't feel like a stranger. As a matter of fact, it seemed as if I had known her for a lifetime. How that happened in such a short span of time was surreal to me, yet it happened and I was going to have to deal with it.

Finally I felt her stir. She shifted on my lap and rose up to look at me. She smiled.

"Sorry."

"Sorry?" I looked at in confusion. I wasn't sure why she was apologizing.

"Yeah…just so you know that was not my intention for coming over here…I wouldn't want you to think I was trying to take advantage of you or anything."

I laughed out loud. "Nah you don't ever have to worry about taking advantage of me. I'm a big boy."

"That you are sir," she smirked. "That you are."

Unable to resist, I rose to give her a brief kiss. Afterwards, she rolled over and started gathering her clothes. I wasn't prepared for her actions so I asked if she leaving. She didn't answer. I reached over and removed the clothes from her hand.

"Stay." She must have sensed my sincerity because she released them without a fight. Tonight I had plans.

I returned to my bedroom and found a t-shirt that I thought would fit her well enough and grabbed a pair of shorts for myself. When I returned I gave her the t-shirt. Even though it almost swallowed her small frame, she still looked sexy as hell wearing it.

Having crossed the line, there was no turning back. I decided that I was going to go all in, starting tonight. "Are you hungry?" I asked. She nodded. I went into the kitchen where I kept an abundant supply of take-out menus in a drawer. I found one for a local bar and grill and called to place an order for sandwiches and wings. I checked my wine supply. Grabbing a bottle of chardonnay, I opened it and quickly poured two glasses. I walked back to the sofa…giving Toni one of them. Then I sat down, turning towards her.

"Let's talk."

And that's exactly what we did, only ceasing long enough to consume the food once it was delivered. We talked about music, art, movies. Her life growing up in rural Georgia, her dream of escaping, her fears, desires, loves. Throughout our conversation, I watched her, loving the light in her eyes whenever she talked about her family and anything related to Muse. Loving the sound of her raspy voice, especially her laugh. Loving her wild hair, her pouty lips.

I touched her, gently stroking her thigh and leg, treasuring its smoothness…softness. I gave her details about growing up in D.C., my childhood with Kyle, the closeness of our family, college-life at Howard. It bothered me that I couldn't tell her about the most important aspect of my life, my daughter, but I didn't want to ruin the evening…it wasn't the right time.

Glancing at the clock I saw that it was getting late. Even though she was fighting, I could see that she was getting tired. I couldn't complain, knowing that she often put in long hours at Muse.

"C'mon lady, you're about to pass out on me," I told her, pulling her up and leading her down the hallway, towards my bedroom.

She pauses momentarily, announcing that she had to work in the morning, however, I wasn't going to be denied. In the middle of her excuses, I tenderly kissed her on the lips. "You're staying," I said firmly, leaving no room for argument. I grabbed her hand and led her into my room. At first, it was weird having her in my space. My bed hadn't been shared with another woman since Sarai and I separated. Once I pulled her into the bed and positioned her body close to mine, any misgivings I had disappeared. This felt right. Toni was exactly where she belonged.

Chapter 8: Could This Be Love?

After two amazing weeks with Keenan, I found myself waking up one Saturday morning with strange feelings. Besides the rare, indescribable ache inside of my body, I also found myself missing him…needing him. The image of his handsome face was a constant presence in my head…minute by minute, I visualized that smile. Each time I thought of him, my heart's reactions led me closer to a conclusion that I wasn't prepared to face… I had fallen in love, maybe. Despite my previous reservations, I smiled. For years I had avoided this feeling as if it was the plague. Not without good reason. Every girl has personal experiences, about the high cost of love…regardless of how good it feels, there's no denying that it often comes at the risk of great loss. Losing control… losing yourself. That wasn't a risk I had been willing to take. I had too much at stake. Yet, here I was, knee-deep in the realization that somehow I was possibly in love with Keenan. Lost in my thoughts, my mind drifted back to the events of the past weeks.

....

That first morning, when I awakened in his bed, was unnerving. The alarm on my phone had gone off, startling me out of an almost coma-like sleep. It took a minute for me to realize that I was not in my own bed. Then, everything about the night before came rushing back. *Keenan*. There he was, still peacefully sleeping, undisturbed by the alarm. I watched him. The sheet was drawn up to his hips, his chest exposed. His lips were slightly parted and he was lightly snoring. His long dreads fell around his shoulders and partially covered his face. My pulse quickened in response to his chocolate beauty. I hated to leave.

Somehow, I managed to escape his apartment undetected. I rushed home, not an easy feat considering Atlanta's morning traffic. I called Mia on the way. Thank God she didn't have an early class and was able to open and manage the store until I was able to make it in. Of course she was curious as to why I would be late, since that was so out of the ordinary for me. I knew I would have to get my mind back on my business.

It ended up being another extremely busy day. We had another event scheduled for that night so I never got the chance to speak with Keenan. However, he managed to keep me heavily distracted by sending random text messages throughout the day…some sweet, telling me how much he missed me…others daringly sexy, expressing how much he wanted to feel me…taste me…lawd I couldn't wait to get those doors locked.

When the event was over, I once again recruited Mia to lock up, not wanting Tanya to ask unwanted questions. As soon as I was in my car, I sped off to Keenan's apartment. He met me at the door, greeting me with tender kisses, which led to soft caresses and eventually, another long night of love making. By Wednesday morning I was no longer unsettled when my alarm awakened me in a stranger's home.

Any available time we had, was spent together. We explored the historical and cultural aspects of the city…visiting tourist staples like the King Center and Underground Atlanta. We also engaged in alternative entertainment like plays at the Horizon Theater. We took extended walks in Piedmont Park and brunched at local diners. Some days, we isolated ourselves in either my house or his apartment, spending countless hours listening to music, watching movies, talking…learning about each other. I have never been happier just to share the same space as another human being. To breathe the same air.

So here I am, on this Saturday morning… my thoughts threatening to overpower me, feeling an unsettling sense of neediness creeping in. I wanted to call him, to hear his voice, to hear him say my name…but I promised myself that I wouldn't. Not today. Clinginess, I firmly reminded myself, is not an attractive trait.

Trying to get a handle on my emotions, I made my way into the kitchen to make a much needed pot of coffee. No, today was not going to be Mr. Jackson's day. I smiled to myself, at least not this morning.

I was definitely losing myself and everyone knew it. I had only seen Rae once in the last couple of weeks and I had been a no-show at our breakfast at Intermezzo. Admittedly, if this was either of them acting a fool about some guy, I would have been the first to give them hell for it. I mean Dawn was even trying to hang out and she was now officially involved with Craig. Though, I don't know if she had this type of intensity with him. She couldn't have, how anyone could function on a daily basis with this type of intense loving was beyond my guess. Perhaps she once had it with Jamie…that fire that she thought would never burn out, dim maybe…but never be fully extinguished… before Lexie, before the arguments, before the misunderstandings. Prior to the divorce, I really didn't know Dawn all that well. Because of her and Rae's friendship, I would often see her and Jamie at events, birthday parties, bowling. Back then, they always seemed to be so much in love. They were *that* couple and she always had a smile and a glow that made the rest of us ladies envious. Where did it all go? How do you have a love like that and it just… disappears?

Keeping this in mind, I once more reminded myself to be cautious with Keenan. Caution is the reason I have survived this long.

Grabbing my cell, I called Rae, rehearsing my apologies as I waited for her to pick up. She answered. "Well lookie here, the dead has arisen." I rolled my eyes even though she couldn't see me. This was not going to be easy. "Hey friend," I simply responded to her sarcasm.

"Oh so you remember that you have friends? Hey Dawn!" I heard her yelling through the phone, "It's a miracle, Toni came out of her coma this morning and remembered her friends." I could hear Dawn laughing in the background, getting in on the foolishness.

"Praises! Praises!" she yelled. Maybe it was my imagination, but I could have sworn that Lexie was even in the background singing it out too. I put my head in my hand, exasperated. Maybe this wasn't such a good idea after all. I needed to make amends, however, it was proving to be a ridiculous task dealing with these two. I put Rae on hold while I went to make a cup of coffee from the freshly brewed pot. Obviously I was going to need it in order to get through this conversation.

"You know what, I'll take that. I deserve it. Forgive me for being MIA these last couple of weeks. As a matter of fact, let me make it up to you both by treating you to a breakfast of your choice, we don't even have to go to Intermezzo." For Dawn, I knew this was a done deal. That chick was not going to pass on anything free, especially a meal, regardless of the situation. Rae, on the other hand, was definitely going to be a tougher nut to crack. I heard her relay my message to Dawn who promptly responded with an expected, "Cool, let me get a babysitter."

One down… one to go. "What's up Rae? I know you're not going to let Dawn get all the scoop with you being left out." This, was her Achilles heel. Being my best friend was a role that Rae took great pride in. Begrudgingly, she shared me with Kyle; however, she was not about to let Dawn be my confidante while she sat on the sidelines watching.

"I guess I'll go," she grumbled. It was a done deal. Dawn was in the background talking, though, I couldn't understand what she was saying. She must have moved further down the hall to begin the process of getting Lexie dressed. This time Rae told me to hold on. When she came back she said that they wanted to go to Murphy's, another one of our favorite spots for breakfast and brunch. We hung up, agreeing to meet in an hour. After a quick shower, I casually dressed in jeans, boots, and a t-shirt. I looked in the mirror, and after weighing my options, decided to allow my hair to breathe from its usual constricting ponytail. Grabbing, my shades and my keys I rushed out of the door, determined to be on time.

....

Brunching at Murphy's must have been at the forefront of many people's minds this morning, as the wait time for three people was at least thirty minutes long. I put us on the waiting list and went to the bar to get a mimosa. It was a nice feeling being first.

Fifteen minutes later, my friends arrived. Like me, Rae was dressed casually…t-shirt, jeans, light summer scarf. Diva, on the other hand was dressed in a heels and a maxi dress, complete with Jacqueline Kennedy-esque shades. Seriously Dawn, I wanted to scream, it was only brunch. We all hugged before I let them know that we had at least another ten minutes before being seated.

I waited by the door, while they went to grab drinks for themselves. Just as they returned, the hostess called my name.

She paraded us through the crowded restaurant and out to the screened-in patio, where we could enjoy the remnants of the early morning light. Up until this point, we had refrained from any detailed conversation, deciding instead to wait until we were seated. I glanced over the menu, quickly deciding to get the French toast and chicken sausage. I quietly observed that it only took a moment for the both of them to decide on their order, either because they were just that hungry or because they were just that anxious to get all in my business.

As soon as our orders were placed, the floodgates opened. Apparently, a lot had been going on in their lives in the weeks of my absence. The most shocking news of the morning was Jamie contacting Dawn for a possible reconciliation. *Unbelievable*. Dawn said he called her out of the blue inviting her to meet him downtown for lunch. After her initial reservations, she decided to go ahead and meet with him. Instantly, his behavior was suspicious. She said he was overly cordial…complimenting her looks, showing his appreciation for the job she was doing with Lexie.

Then, as we love to say, the foolishness began. He started reminiscing about their life together, about the moments he missed with her and Lexie as a family. She hadn't seen him be that sincere and emotional in a long time. After his confession, he humbly asked if he could have another chance…to prove his worth as a husband, a father. She was speechless. And so were we. Rae and I had front row seats to Jamie and Dawn's soap opera so we knew better than anyone how much hell he has put her through. Not only was he neglecting Lexie, Dawn also discovered, that he had been saying some very hurtful things. Telling friends he wasn't sure if he ever loved her, and that he was feeling as if their marriage was suffocating him.

In some ways his feelings were legitimate. They were married at an early age after meeting and dating in college. After graduation, Jamie started an entry-level position at accounting firm while Dawn found a position at a bank. For several years they were like any other young professional black couple in Atlanta…trying to accomplish big dreams. Then, it all came tumbling down. Jamie's company was challenged by financial difficulties and, in time, did a massive lay-off. When the dust finally settled, Jamie, unfortunately, was among the numerous casualties. After losing his job, he sank into a deep depression and appeared to lose sight of who he was. At first, he wouldn't even leave the house, choosing instead to either sit around watching television or simply sleep. Dawn, ultimately, started showing up at events without him and the glow that used to be ever-present on her face began to fade.

In Jamie's next phase of joblessness, he began hanging out with his friends all day every day. He was a constant patron of the local bars and clubs as if his marital status changed along with his employment status. Dawn would beg him to spend more time with Lexie, but it was like he was going through some sort of early mid-life crisis…he disconnected from their world. She ended up getting a part-time job to assist with the mounting bills. Jamie, was too prideful to do so. Being from an upper-class, established family in Atlanta, he didn't want his friends and family to see him doing "menial" jobs. On the other hand, Dawn was from Detroit, and was a natural born hustler. Early in life, she had weathered the foster care system, so surviving in tough times was second nature. It greatly disappointed her that her husband, who was supposed to be her partner in life, could not get it together and step up as a man when she and Lexie needed him the most.

…….

Surviving , in due time, meant walking away and filing for divorce. Never did she think that her daughter would be subjected to the same broken home that she endured. She hated Jamie for their circumstances.

Now, he was back, begging for a second chance. The unspoken question … what she was going to do about it? To be honest, it was already shocking to me that she hadn't cursed him out and sent him back to the pit out of which he crawled.

"So what are you thinking?" I cautiously asked. She looked at me with confusion resting in her eyes. "Honestly Toni, I don't know. I mean, if it was just me, then my answer would be a resounding 'No!', then I think about Lexie. She misses her daddy. At least the father she once knew. And I want her to have her family because not having mine…well," her voice trailed off. She didn't have to say anything else. We knew her story…the hardship she suffered growing up. A dad, who deserted her mom, a mom who became a drug addict, often neglecting her three children for the call of the streets and her relentless urge to get high. Three children that became wards of the state of Michigan because no family members wanted the additional financial burden of raising them. One little girl, now a woman determined not to repeat history. Yes, my friend was truly carrying a heavy load.

Rae finally broke the tension, "Hey, girl whatever you decide to do you know we will be there for you as always. You are an awesome woman and I know you will make the right decision for you and Lexie. Jamie doesn't even deserve you. He should be grateful that you're even thinking about taking his sorry ass back." Dawn and I both laughed. As usual, the pit bull was ready for battle.

"Right!" Dawn stated. "Anyway, we've spent enough time talking about my ex-husband. I need to get what I really came for…Ms. Toni, what's up with you? Where have you been or better yet, who have you been with, because it sure hasn't been with your friends."

I knew it was coming. There would be no avoiding it. Before I dove into the details of my lust life, I ordered coffee. Rae was already sitting close to the table, her small face resting on her folded hands. Waiting for me to answer. I did. I provided the full details of the last couple of weeks with Keenan; the time spent together, the love made together, the conversations shared. I knew I sounded like a high school teenager with a massive crush but I didn't care. And judging by the looks on their faces, they were just as excited as I was.

I finished my monologue and for a minute, neither of them spoke. They just sat there staring at me as if a spaceship had just landed and dropped me off in the middle of the restaurant.

"What's the matter with you two?" I asked, growing tired of the silence. They looked at each other before Dawn started laughing. Not the reaction I was expecting. Shaking my head, I looked at Rae, who I could tell was also trying to hold herself together.

"Are you serious? I can't believe y'all heifers are laughing. What the hell is so funny?" By this time other people in the restaurant had begun to look in our direction. This was embarrassing and I was becoming angry. I slapped Dawn on the hand and told her to shut up. Finally she calmed down and apologized.

"Girl I'm sorry, but I don't think I have *ever* heard you talk about a man like that. Seriously, that brother must have put something on you." As soon as she finished, Rae started giggling. "She's right Toni, I didn't think that you would get caught up this fast but girl you are really falling for this man. Could it be that Ms. Toni has finally found love?"

That same question I was just asking myself. Was it really possible to fall in love with someone after just a few weeks? Truthfully, I can't even say for certain that I am in love with Keenan. What I do know is that for the first time ever in a relationship I feel alive. Whenever I'm with him, it's as if my world is more illuminated. In his presence, my mind becomes more aware of the feel of my own skin, the taste and feel of his. The beauty of us seems to increase and expand into the landscape around us. Colors are brighter, sounds are more piercing. Could this be love? I couldn't say for sure. However you define it, I know that it is an essential piece that has been missing from my life and now that I've found it, I plan on keeping it.

Our food finally arrived. The conversation ceased, as we consumed our meals. Then Rae approached another sensitive subject. Kyle. Had I told him about me and Keenan? Of course I hadn't. The coward in me had not allowed that conversation to take place. Once Keenan and I realized that we would be spending more time together, we knew Kyle would eventually have to be told, but how and by whom were the logistics that we just couldn't seem to figure out. Either way, he was not going to be pleased. Not that I could blame him. Putting myself in his shoes, I don't think I would be overjoyed to have my cousin and best friend in a relationship or having sex. It's all good as long as it's all good, but what happens to all involved if things go wrong. *Greg and Shana.* Awkward situations can sometimes never be made right again.

Dawn rolled her eyes. She didn't understand why I felt the need to answer to Kyle or anyone else being that I am, as she so often claims, "A grown ass woman." She never would though, because she has always been fiercely independent.

"Seriously Toni I know how close you and Kyle are, but you don't owe him your life. Take my word for it, Kyle is going to do some serious cock-blocking and you are going to be all sensitive to his needs and find yourself right back where you started…alone."

Did she really just call Kyle a cock-blocker? Shaking my head, I stared back at her. Dawn is insane. Kyle can be a little tough on the guys I date, but that's not cock-blocking, it's only because he genuinely cares about me and doesn't want to see me getting hurt. She wasn't finished.

"I don't even know why you two are looking at me all crazy like that. If you haven't figured out by now that no man is *ever* going to be good enough for Toni in Kyle's eyes, well then you're the ones crazy…and blind. Kyle thinks *he's* the perfect man for Toni."

Rae added her thoughts. "Dawn that's some foolishness. You're just trying to start some stuff. Don't go ruining the girl's moment by throwing in some random red herring that has nothing to do with the situation. Look Toni, you really are going to have to talk to Kyle if you and Keenan are becoming serious. That's only fair, considering he will be affected. He's going to be all wrapped up in his little feelings for a minute, but he'll be ok. You deserve to be happy. Hell we all deserve to be happy. Can we toast to that?"

We laughed in unison as we held up our mimosas toasting to what we hoped would be brighter days and more promising tomorrows. As my glass chimed with Dawn's, I pushed her warning to the far corners of my mind.

Chapter 9: Confessions

Could my life get any more complicated? For weeks I have been trying to avoid Kyle. Today, there would be no way around it. He called and invited me to lunch and, since I wasn't doing anything of significance, I agreed to go. Besides, he knew me better than anyone, so he would have known if any last minute excuse I managed to come up with rang false.

I coaxed him into picking me up from the apartment. Hurriedly, I showered and dressed in my favorite t-shirt and jeans. My eyes did a quick scan of the room for my keys and wallet, both of which I located near the bar. I went through the usual process of checking for my cash and cards, a simple routine established long ago during the course of my marriage.

Pausing for a minute, I reflected back to happier, normal times, when life was just as simple as everyday routines... heading out of the house, checking for my keys and wallet...making sure the alarm was set. Sarai, getting jackets, turning off lights, and grabbing all necessities associated with keeping Zy'riah occupied and entertained ...toys, games, stuffed animals, snacks. Alarms, drop offs, bedtime stories, wind downs. Sometimes memories like these free themselves from my subconscious, leaving me breathless. Closing my eyes I lived in the memory, admitting to myself that I missed them, especially my daughter. The situation is more complicated with Sarai...certainly the good times are missed, nevertheless, there's no denying the bad times. I sure haven't made the situation any easier by getting involved with Toni. This I know. I kissed a picture of my baby girl before sliding the wallet and keys into my front pocket.

The doorbell rang, announcing Kyle's arrival. Despite the circumstances, I'm actually glad that we are getting a chance to hang out. It's been minute, and, I'll accept the blame for that. If I'm not working on a piece, I'm spending time with Toni. It was never my intention for her to become so entrenched in my world but hey, it is what it is.

Kyle noisily made his entrance. "What's up cousin…man I thought we would see more of each other when you moved here but you have pulled a classic disappearing act on me…where the hell have you been?"

Sighing I grabbed my jacket as we headed out of the door towards his waiting all black BMW. He must have had a meeting because his "baby" only comes out for special occasions. If he's just running errands he would drive his Tacoma pickup. My cousin was definitely enjoying the spoils of being an attorney.

Although for him, being that attorney has proven to be his greatest blessing, it has often been a curse to close friends and family, who have to withstand his inquisitions and interrogations on all matters personal and otherwise. Like now. I know there will be a barrage of questions hitting me and he will not stop until he gets the answers he's looking for. My plan is to give him those answers because I was done hiding.

He drove to Millie's, a BBQ and blues joint near my apartment. Remarkably, Kyle didn't ask a lot of questions on the way. Then again, it's only 10 minutes away from the apartment so maybe he just decided to wait. The usual crowd had not yet arrived. We found seats without much of a hassle. A live band was scheduled for later in the evening and then it would be standing room only. Millie's is one of those places described as a "hole in the wall." The décor consisted of a variety of wooden chairs and tables, adorned with standard and cheap checkered table cloths. Should you happen to find yourself dining when there wasn't a live band, you could always find a selection of old school song choices from the 60's through 80's era on the aged jukebox in the corner. The actual stage was no more than a black platform located in the front of the restaurant. Depending on how large the band was, it was not unusual find the members practically sitting in your lap. Not an upscale establishment, but the food was delicious and the atmosphere could get lively with dancing, sweating, and hollering.

I loved it. I made a mental note to bring Toni the next Friday night she was free. We ordered and I turned to Kyle, ready to get this conversation over and done with. Before he could ask any questions, I blurted out that I was seeing Toni. Then, I watched the emotional reactions form on his face, shifting from shock, to hurt and disappointment, and finally, anger. The anger was the part that would be our biggest obstacle. I just hoped our bond was strong enough to overcome it.

Still speechless. This was unnatural for Kyle. I wanted to say something, but I knew he needed space to process what I just told him. There was so much to it than words.

At last he spoke, his voice choked with emotions.

"You know, when you walked out of the club with her that night I wanted so badly to run after you because that girl, man, that girl is my best friend and I have spent a good portion of my life protecting her. I prayed that it would be for one night, but my heart knew differently because I *know* her. She is easy to love and my heart kept saying if he knows her he is going to love her and he can't love her. He can't love her because he is married and he has a daughter. So surely he will make the right decision and not *love* her because if he does that, then she will love him back. And it is inevitable that he will fail her. I'm thinking my brother would not do that to my best friend. *Yet*...here we are Keenan. Here we are."

What could I say? Of course he was right. That first night when I met Toni, I realized that she could be trouble for me. I knew it when we left the club together that night. Not that I had been on my best behavior since arriving in Atlanta... there had been a few dates and I had even slept with another female, so I won't claim innocence. Foolishly, I thought Toni would be just...fun. Kyle was right. I should have known better. Based on everything he's always told me about her, I should have known better and I should have been prepared. Or better yet, I should have left well enough alone.

My interest in Toni had been piqued long before I ever met her. By Kyle's junior year in college, she was all that he spoke of, to a point that I thought he was actually dating her. Toni was beautiful. Toni was smart. Toni was funny. However, whenever I questioned him about her in more detail, he always brushed me off, stating that she was more like his little sister and he never thought of her that way. Somehow I was never really convinced.

Our food arrived and we ate in silence. I'm sorry that he's angry, but my heart is lighter, having revealed the secret. I only hoped this revelation wouldn't impact our relationship. Kyle is more than my cousin, he is my brother. The two of us, the only children of sisters, forged a bond at an early age that still exists. We have been through everything together...he stood with me as the best man at my wedding. I literally held him together when my aunt died. There's no way we can't get beyond this.

The conversation eventually picked up again and with it more questions. Did Toni know about me being married? No. Did Sarai know about my relationship with Toni? Nope. Exasperation was evident on his face.

"Keenan, what the hell are you doing man? Do you even realize what you have done to me? You have put *me* right in the middle of *your* storm. Toni is my best friend. Sarai is like my sister. This is crazy. Are you planning on getting a divorce or what?"

I wish I had answers to his questions but I didn't. The direction in which my marriage was headed was still a mystery, even to me, but I couldn't allow my feelings for Toni to factor into the equation. Besides, I didn't even know where we were headed. Then there was my daughter. If nothing else, I felt like I owed my daughter a life with both of her parents present. My own parents have remained married for years, even through the difficult times. Many of my close friends haven't been as lucky. I've witnessed their horror stories of divorce. Broken promises, anger…abandonment. I didn't want that for my daughter. No, there were no easy answers to this.

....

We finished eating and decided to head to Lenox Mall. There were no more discussions about Toni or Sarai, although, I knew the subject was not forgotten. Since we hadn't seen each other in a minute, we didn't want the day to be completely ruined. Kyle loosened up and we were able to laugh and joke like old times. The peaches were out in full force, which, helped to keep him in a good mood. The weather was beautiful, hot, but not stifling…a signal for all of the sundresses, halter tops, and booty shorts to get pulled from their storage bins and put on full display.

I've been out enough with Kyle to know that the game has changed since my long-ago single days. Back then we chose. Now, females are clearly choosing. And it's apparent that their choices are increasingly based on financial status, cars, and everything else material. Kyle, the golden boy, is often chosen. Between his looks, his Movado watches, and his BMW, he always catches someone's eye and they work extra hard to catch his.

Today was no different. We were waiting in line at Starbuck's when this young slim beauty in a black sundress crossed our path for the third time. We almost laughed out loud when we saw her again. There it was.

She got in line behind us and gave us a small smile. Up close she was even prettier. She was tall, taller than my taste, and slim. I could tell from her arms and shoulders that she was either an athlete or worked out consistently. Her skin was the color of honey, a stark contrast to her hair, which she had obviously dyed jet black. It hung to her shoulders in soft curls. *Nice.*

I paid for a regular cup of coffee and stepped to the side. Kyle placed his order and without hesitation turned to ask the young lady what she was having. Without missing a step, she smiled and ordered a venti cappuccino. Just like that, I knew our day was about to come to an abrupt end. I walked over to view some sneakers, giving them a moment to talk. My phone rang just as I was about to walk into the store. *Toni.*

"Hey you." I whispered into the phone. "Hey back," she answered in her usual greeting. I could hear the smile in her voice. I have to admit, it is a damn good feeling knowing that I was the man putting that smile on her face.

"What are you doing?" I asked.

"Missing you", she replied, and I could tell from the husky tone of her voice that she was in a sexy kind of mood. My body instantly responded. *Damn I loved that voice.*

"Girl don't play with me like this. How you going to get all sexy on me on our day off. That's just not right."

Glancing around, I noticed that Kyle was still distracted. I located an isolated table in the corner of the food court to hold this conversation in private.

"What do you mean? I'm not playing with you. I am missing you. You know it's really not fair that I'm home all alone, relaxing in this luxurious bath, drinking my chilled chardonnay…all by myself."

She was actually going to do this. As she spoke, my mind formulated vivid images from her words. I could imagine her brown skin slippery, shimmering, and wet from a combination of water and oils. I could almost feel its slickness, silkiness through the phone. This was so not good. I shifted uncomfortably in my seat and conducted a quick scan of the area to see if there were any bystanders wandering nearby.

"I certainly don't want you to feel lonely babe. I wish I was right there with you right now."

"I think I'm going to need you tonight baby. I'm aching right now…I miss you so much. I need you here…kissing me…touching me…stroking me…ummm." She moaned into the phone and I swear I felt her breath on my neck. I shifted again. If she kept this up this was going to be an embarrassing situation. This girl was driving me insane. I had to get to her.

"Baby hold that thought, I'm going to call you right back." I hung up the phone before she could even answer. I did a quick search for Kyle, who by now was sitting at a table with his new friend. I took three minutes to calm down before walking over to where he was. I hated to interrupt, but this was a desperate situation.

"Hey man, sorry to interrupt, but I have to bounce. You don't have to rush, I can catch MARTA."

Kyle looked up with a surprised expression on his face, as if he had forgotten that I was even with him. Typical. I let him know that it wasn't an emergency but something came up that I needed to take care of. Even though his eyes were full of questions, I knew that he wouldn't ask them with a stranger present. He looked to his "friend" before turning back towards me.

"No you don't have to catch MARTA man, we can just go. I'm good. Stacy, I will give you a call later ok." Stacy disappeared and once more it was just the two of us.

He turned to me, "Aiight so what's this emergency that's come up all of a sudden. It better be something serious. Did you see her? Did you get a good look at that female who just walked away? I mean I know you saw that ass right?"

Not wanting to play games with him I simply stated that I was going to see Toni. His entire body stiffened.

"Damn man, seriously…so not one word I said to you today got through. You're just going to continue to have a relationship with my best friend knowing that you're married… regardless of how I feel?"

I didn't feel the need to answer him. Although I respect Kyle, our relationship, I'm not going to let him or anyone else control my life. I had already jumped into the fire so now I was going to see how long I could stand the heat. Tension hung in the air, thicker even than words. After a minute, he sighed and said let's go.

There was no conversation on the way to Toni's. Kyle's body language expressed his frustration. Not wanting to push him I remained silent. I did call Toni back to let her know that I was on the way. Speaking to her only served to amplify my excitement so I tried to forget about Kyle pouting in the seat beside me. Within 30 minutes we were there. I prayed that he wouldn't try to get out to see Toni. This definitely wasn't the right time. But when he pulled up, he never turned the car off so I knew he wasn't trying to stay. As I got out of the car, I turned back to him and gave him a quiet thank-you. I knew we would be ok when he silently nodded back. Then he drove off and I turned my attention to the woman I came to see.

....

I rang the doorbell, barely containing my excitement. At this point I was just ready to wrap myself all around her. When she answered the door, I stepped in and was instantly taken aback. There she was, standing completely naked in the middle of the room. Her mess of curls formed a halo around her head. Her body was glistening and shimmering in the soft glow of candles that were lit around the room. There was no make-up on her face, only a trace of lip gloss on her luscious lips. A song I didn't recognize was playing in the background. Listening to the voice, I could tell that it was Donny Hathaway. A blanket was spread on the floor and she already had a bottle of wine chilling in a bucket with ice. She never spoke. She just stood there staring at me with her big brown eyes so full of emotion that it caught me off guard. I wasn't sure what to do with all of it. And being in the midst of it all scared me. No words spoken…so much revealed. She opened her arms. At that moment, I wanted nothing more than to love this woman who was giving herself to me without inhibitions or restraint. The best gift a man could ask for.

I quickly shed my clothes and glided into her waiting arms. I pressed her full body against mine. Her warmth, her softness a perfect contrast to the hardness of my own body. I found her mouth, wet and waiting. She moaned as I passionately kissed her. I grabbed her hair pulling her into me as I greedily sucked at her lips, her tongue. The more of her I tasted, the more I wanted. After some time, I pulled away. Both of gasped for air. She was unsteady on her feet, so I eased her down on the blanket. With her back slightly arched her nipples prominently stood out, erect from excitement. I couldn't resist.

I deliberately licked one, then the other, one then the other. She cried out my name, her first words since allowing me to enter the house. I was in a frantic battle with myself not to lose control. I touched her face and she opened her eyes to look at me.

"Is this what you wanted baby?" She nodded then gave me a quiet "yes."

Gazing down at her lovely face, I told her that I was going to love her tonight. I meant every word. I knew I should be holding back, not giving her this much of me, but there was an overwhelming urge to pour myself into her...an urge greater than my sense of caution. This would have to be fixed, but not tonight. Tonight I needed to love her.

She whimpered as total comprehension dawned on her. I kissed her briefly on the lips then started a trail of kisses down her chest, her stomach, and her inner thighs. Her legs quivered as I got closer to the center of her heat. The sweet smell of her was driving me insane. *Love her.*

With slow strokes, I used my tongue to caress the folds of her womanhood. She reached for my hair in an attempt to pull me deeper...I resisted. Her taste was as sweet as her smell. I licked her intensely...she screamed my name louder. I found her clit and started my loving assault there. Licking, sucking...nibbling. She bathed me in her juices, but I refused to stop until she gave me everything. I grabbed her ass, pressing her into me. Her grip on my hair got tighter. She bucked against me but I held firm until she let out one long wail. I knew that she was cumming. I held her tightly until she came down from her explosive climax.

No more screams...only soft cries. Yet, I wasn't finished. I turned her over on her stomach. She moved without much resistance. Slowly, I entered her from behind. She gasped...I moaned. Damn she was so slick...so warm. I was still for a minute trying to gain control of my body…rejoicing in the fact that I was within her…connected to this beautiful soul. I began making love to her in long slow strokes. I could still hear her soft cries, which made it even more difficult. I kissed her back, caressed her hair. She joined me in the dance slowly grinding back against me…forming a perfect union. With each stroke, my swollen manhood was gripped tightly by her pulsating walls. I filled her completely, claiming her body as my own possession. Before long, I was completely lost. My thrusts became faster, harder, deeper. Her cries became louder as she wildly bucked against me. Moaning her name I grabbed her ripe ass and began pounding into her until my body became weak and I erupted forcefully inside of her. I collapsed on top of her breathing heavily. My cascading coils formed a snake-like curtain across her sweating back.

Within five minutes, she was asleep. I withdrew from her and went in search of a blanket. When I returned, I stood for a moment and watched her sleep. The last few weeks have been an amazing journey getting to know this woman. She was a beautiful and complicated spirit. In that instant I realized she had done what no other woman had before or since I first met Sarai…captured my heart. How did I get here?

I covered her with the blanket and went to take a shower, thoughts still crowding my mind. The water, running through my hair and over my body, was soothing. This wasn't fair to her. I couldn't deny that. What was I thinking? This was an impossible situation. My old life still held me captive. As a result, I couldn't move forward. At this point, however, I didn't know how to let her go. Kyle was right…a perfect storm was brewing and there was no way to avoid the casualties. The question was, who would be left standing when the dust settled?

Chapter 10: Melancholy Mood

Another week, another Saturday morning. I needed peace. I sat in the corner of my favorite booth…coffee already in hand. I only heard from Keenan once, which left me puzzled. When I awakened last Saturday night, I was startled to find him, not only awake, but in a melancholic mood. The bottle of wine was almost empty. He was sitting on the floor next to me, his back against the sofa. He turned towards me when he heard me stir. There was sadness in his eyes.

"Hey you" I said hoping to break the tension.

"Hey back." At least he gave me a small smile. Why this pain when the night had been full of so much pleasure? He must have seen the questions in my eyes because he leaned forward and kissed my forehead then softly on the lips.

"Read for me" he softly requested. Sometimes, during our long nights together, we would open up to each other, sharing pieces of ourselves. Never before had I established that routine with anyone else…then again, I've never been with someone who was this open and giving of themselves. I wanted to match what he gave. Thus, there were moments when I would watch him during his creative process and I, in turn, would share my favorite poems or, on very rare occasions, share ones that I had actually written.

"You want a little Nikki?" I asked in reference to one of my favorite poets Nikki Giovanni.

"No." He quietly stated. "I want all of you."

He passed me the notebook that I normally keep on the nightstand. Sensing his need, I turned to one that I had written specifically about him after another long, wonderful night.

DEFINITION:

I would call you an ENIGMA...

But that word seems too mundane and shallow

To accurately describe

The complex structure of your nature...

I would say that you are BEAUTIFUL:

Yet that doesn't seem to be a just portrayal of

The flawless texture of your skin

The godly curves of your physique

The Adonis quality of your smile

The artistic angles of your face

Can I call you DELECTABLE?

That would seem to me

A more righteous description

Especially when I think about the

Honey drippings

From your tongue

The succulent fullness of your mouth

The sweet and salty taste of your love...

What I do know is that you are ABSTRACT:

Each elemental piece

Complicated in its design

Yet the sum of your whole parts

Is the creation of an intricate being that is...

Perfection...

I closed the book and looked at him waiting for his reaction. At first, he didn't say anything. Then quietly he spoke. "You are amazing."

Now... nothing. And to say I'm confused is an understatement. What happened to make him withdraw? A tap on the glass pane ended my reverie. *Kyle.*

I opened the door, instantly offering a hug. I didn't want to let go. The contact was welcoming.

"Hey friend."

"Hey love, what's wrong?"

What could I say? This was the part of dating your best friend's cousin that made the situation awkward. I glanced at him before wordlessly walking back to my booth.

"Oh ok." He went to make himself a cup of coffee and squeezed in beside me. "Look, I already know what's up so you might as well talk. Sitting here looking like a lost puppy."

I laughed, glad that he had come by. I had missed him. I realized that I was so caught up in Keenan that my relationship with him was being neglected, again. I'm sure he's not pleased about it.

"I love him." There was no reason to lie about it. At some point, I stopped denying the blatant truth even to myself.

"Ah Toni, why doesn't that surprise me." I thought he would be angry; instead, he seemed more resigned. Actually, he seemed sad too. What the hell was going on?

"Kyle, I don't understand. I felt like we were on the same page, especially this past weekend. Then, this emotional shift. He started pulling away without an explanation. I've been waiting for him to come over, but he keeps blowing me off. He's only called once. I don't know, it's just driving me crazy. I don't know what to do. I don't understand why it even has to be this complicated."

I was looking to him for some type of answer or explanation but he seemed as if he was struggling to come up with words. *Strange.* Kyle has never been speechless regarding my personal business. He always has an opinion and, even though this circumstance involved Keenan, he would still be just as vocal. A sense of fear crept along my spine.

"Kyle is there something going on that I should know about? Is he seeing someone else? " I don't know why it hadn't occurred to me that another female could be in the picture. It didn't seem possible since pretty much all of our free time was spent with each other, then again, we've never confirmed that were exclusively dating either. This would be my worst nightmare.

"Toni, I can't believe you and Keenan have put me in this situation. The last thing I want is to be in the middle of anything going on between you two. But your ass is always so stubborn." He turned to face me. "Let me ask you a question. Can you not love him? If I begged you right now to walk away from him, could you do that?"

Why was he asking me this? Without warning, tears formed in my eyes. I shook my head. He sighed and pulled out his phone. Still staring at me, he stated "Keenan, I am here with Toni. You have to tell her the truth or I will. She's on her way over." He hung up the phone and said that he would stay in the store until Tanya got there and for me to go ahead and leave. I didn't know what to do. Somehow I knew that in less than thirty minutes my life would completely change and I wasn't sure that I was ready for it. I felt as though I was moving in quicksand, as I got up to get my purse and head out of the door. As I headed out, I heard Kyle speak my name. I stopped without looking back.

"I will be here."

....

I couldn't believe what I was hearing. My mind processed the rest of his words as garbled, incoherent sounds. *Married.* No. Please Keenan don't do this to me...don't be every enemy my heart has always been afraid of. I closed my eyes, hoping that when I opened them I would awaken from this unforeseen nightmare. *Married.* I couldn't breathe. I opened my eyes but Keenan was still there, throwing daggers with his tongue, every word a short, quick stab into this dream that I've created.

"You let me fall in love with you." I spit the words at him, cutting him off in midsentence. My voice was raspy, a mixture of pain and anger. For a minute, we just stared at each other, unblinking. He was the first to look away, maybe in an attempt to hide his shame, or perhaps he no longer wanted to witness the full onslaught of emotions on my face.

A searing headache was beginning to form at my right temple. This couldn't possibly be happening. Not to me...not to the girl who painstakingly built a massive emotional wall brick by brick. The irony of the situation seemed...cruel.

"Why?" I found myself asking, even though, subconsciously, I knew that I wasn't going to get the answer I was searching for.

"Why Keenan?" I asked again, "Why did you let this masquerade go on for so long? How could you...with everything you came to know about me...of me...I don't get it."

He rubbed his hand across his face. This, a usual reaction from him whenever he's frustrated. Funny, only moments ago, it was one of his familiar gestures that I loved. Still loved. Now I'm realizing that we were never supposed to be that familiar.

Finally he spoke. Some words I expected. Saying that he never meant to hurt me. How he never expected the situation to get this far out of control. Others I wasn't prepared for...him telling me that he never expected to fall for me the way that he has...how if I gave him a second chance he would try to make this right.

Try? There will be no *trying* to make this situation right. The damage had been done as soon as the words "I'm married" rolled off of his tongue and glided through his lips. Did he really think that there would be anything to salvage from this mess he created. This hurt is by no means superficial and it won't heal quickly. Tears pooled in my eyes before spilling over onto my cheeks. I was still in a state of disbelief. Spoon by spoon he had fed me the dream that we had a future together. For the first time, I had allowed myself look beyond the present… to envision the possibility of kids, a home, the rocking chairs on the front porch. I saw that in him because he allowed me to think that it was possible. If he would've held back then maybe I would've recognized the warnings. Instead, he *loved* me. I felt everything that he gave…his vulnerability, strength, passion. How could he give all of that to me knowing that he had a wife? A woman who already possessed the blueprint to his future. Shaking my head, I thought to myself, no Mr. Jackson, this could not be fixed.

My mind tuned back in only to realize that the nightmare had gotten even worse.

"Toni, did you hear me?" Keenan was asking. Of course I didn't. How could I with this thick cloud of fog now occupying every space in my head.

"I have more to tell you." I looked at him then and realized that he looked even more anguished than before. Really? God help me. Could I possibly survive this ordeal?

"I have a child. A five-year old daughter, Zy'riah."

The headache now existed in both temples and threatened to become a full blown migraine.

A *child*. Another woman had his baby. I stood up to leave knowing that if I stayed, I would physically assault him. Although I loved him, I was not willing to risk the loss of everything that I've worked for. I was cutting my losses before the wounds got any deeper…I was letting go.

"Toni please stay and let me explain."

I turned back, "Stay Keenan? How can I stay in a place where I don't belong? You tell me where there is a place for me in all of this. You have a *family*. You already wear the roles of husband and…father…who or what could you possibly be to me?"

He came to where I was standing. I was too weary to move. He made a futile attempt to wipe away the tears that were still flowing. "Toni, I understand if you no longer want to be with me, but I need for you to understand that I loved you…love you…me and Sarai have been separated and leading different lives even before I moved here with Kyle. I never expected to find you and once I did, I knew there was no way I could lose you. Nonetheless I can't lose my daughter either…she's my life, she's everything. I just don't know what to do."

Every part of me wanted so badly to believe in him. At the end of the day, though, his words held little meaning. His marriage was an unresolved matter and until it was, I couldn't be a part of the equation. With a heavy heart, I removed his hand from my face, holding onto it a little longer just for comfort, before letting go.

"Keenan, I really don't have any doubts about your love for me…but selfishly, you didn't give me a choice to be involved in this life. So I have to look out for me…and I'm choosing to walk away."

I dropped his hand, grabbed my purse and walked out of his door and out of his life. I felt the cracks in my wounded heart extending with each step. This time he didn't try to stop me.

Chapter 11: The Business of Living

Two days, maybe three, time lost. I lay in bed not moving or eating…feeling numb. Needing to ease the all-consuming pain in my body…not knowing where to begin. Still crying, still in disbelief. Hating, loving…always aching. I briefly spoke to Tanya and told her that I was sick and would be out for a few days. From the sound of her voice, I could tell she was concerned…I had never been out of the store for more than two days at a time since we opened. I told her to call Mia, who would love to pick up some extra hours.

Keenan must have spoken to Kyle because he called me more than once. But I couldn't talk to him, couldn't face him. Kyle must have spoken to Rae because she called me consistently and I could hear the sense of urgency in her voice on the voicemails. I couldn't face her either. There was shame in knowing that I had been a fool.

No calls from Keenan, not that I expected any. Or maybe I did. Maybe I still expected him to call me, to check on me, to see the damage that he was responsible for. But there was nothing. And that empty void was painful. In spite of it all, I missed him. Missed his voice, his presence, his body. Even in just a few short days I felt as if I was going through withdrawal. My body yearned for him and the ache was sometimes unbearable. How was I going to get through this?

I rolled out of bed and staggered into the bathroom. I didn't recognize the person staring back at me from the mirror. My hair was a tangled mess, eyes puffy and red, clothes dirty that I had slept in for two, maybe three days. I brushed my teeth and put cool water on my face. Progress.

Just as I was heading back to the bedroom, the doorbell rang. Really? I wasn't going to answer it until my cell rang and I saw that it was Kyle. I answered. He was outside and was not going away. *Damn.* I dragged myself to the door and unlocked it. Before he could make a complete entrance, I was already back to my bedroom. I heard his footsteps behind me but I didn't stop until I found the sanctuary of my room and bed. I pulled the covers over my head, willing the darkness to swallow me up. I could feel Kyle hovering in the doorway. Sense him when he moved closer to the bed. Then …the crackling of paper bags disturbed the peace of my solitude. There would be no more hiding today.

He spoke. "Toni. I brought some food because I knew you would be in this house half dead from starvation and neglect. Get up." Unceremoniously, he yanked the covers away from my head. I turned and glared at him, willing him to disappear.

"Today, my friend, you will get back to the business of living." That look was in his eyes. That look of determination and stubbornness he gets whenever he is working on a difficult case…when he refuses to concede defeat to his opponent. It was all there…for me…and me knowing my best friend, he would not be satisfied until he had me back on my feet and ready to battle the world again. I couldn't fight him. Not now. For now, I was willing to let him win.

I sighed and sat up in the bed, curiously looking at the bags that I hadn't noticed when he first walked in. My stomach viciously reacted to the scents that were now attacking my nostrils. When was my last meal? I couldn't remember being that I was so wrapped up in my emotions.

Kyle left briefly to go get my bed tray. He made quick work of preparing the food on paper plates. The meal consisted of BBQ chicken, beans, potato salad, and sweet tea, a southern feast for my starving body. Just looking at it made me ravenous. Once he was finished, he didn't have to beg me to eat. I was more than ready. Although there was much to discuss, we ate the entire meal in silence.

When we finished, he wordlessly gathered all of the leftovers and trash and headed back to the kitchen. I heard the refrigerator and cabinet doors opening and closing. I deduced that he was looking for containers to store the food in. He was meticulous like that. After a few minutes he returned, took off his shoes at the door, and climbed into bed with me, wrapping me all up in his love. This was the reason he was my best friend. There were no words of chastisement, no scolding…he knew exactly what I needed. Love with no conditions. I laid my head on his chest and without warning, hot tracks of tears began flowing down my face. There was inconsolable pain in my heart. I wanted to love Keenan. I wanted him in my life. I wanted him to love me back. I did not want this. For years I had tried desperately to avoid it, yet here I was. In this place of misery and pain. Why would he do this to me?

Kyle softly stroked my hair, while I kept my face buried in his chest. The smell and familiarity of his cologne was comforting. I was ashamed at how I had casually dismissed him when Keenan came into the picture. He didn't deserve it and I felt as if I didn't deserve this kindness and comfort he was giving to me now. Even though Keenan was his cousin, he was still here, giving his best effort to dull this ache he knew I was experiencing. I appreciated him for that and I was thankful.

Time passed. At some point my tears ceased without me even being aware of it. I shifted away from the comfort of Kyle's chest, sitting up on the bed, indicating to him that I was ready to talk. And finally I was ready…hiding from the world proved to be futile anyway…the pain was still there and at the end of the day I was just going to have to learn how to deal with it. The only thing left to do now was to try to get answers as to how it could have all happened in the first place. One question that had been nagging me since finding out about Keenan's other life was why Kyle didn't tell me. I know that I pushed him away when Keenan and I became serious, but I was his best friend…he should have told me whether I wanted to hear it, accept it or not. Instead, he said nothing. And here I am. That may not be fair to him, but it's where I am mentally.

So I asked him pointedly, why the silence when I needed his loud objections the most. He looked away briefly before candidly answering.

"Toni, I love you. I probably love you more than you even know, but this was a choice I had to make between you and family. I was praying that you and Keenan wouldn't get serious, that somehow you would just stay in your little box, but I should have known better. And I didn't know how to tell you about his life. That was a choice he had to make. Those are his complications and you were each other's choices. Once I saw how deep you had fallen for him that's when I decided to give him the ultimatum. I'm just sorry this happened. Sorry for your hurt. Sorry for his. Sorry for this situation."

Keenan's hurt? Was he serious? He created this mess. I still didn't, couldn't understand how he could choose me when he was already chosen. What gave him the right to do that? What gave him the right to make me love him, when he knew damn well I couldn't?

"Forgive me if I don't exhibit any sympathy for any so-called hurt that Keenan Jackson may be feeling," I stated angrily. "I'm just a little too pre-occupied nursing my own wounds."

Kyle laughed softly. "Toni, trust me if anyone knows how you can be whenever you're all wrapped up in your feelings, it's me. I've cleaned my share of your wounds remember. And trust me, I was more than angry with Keenan when I realized you guys had progressed to a 'relationship'. I would have expected better from him. But that man is hurting, believe me on that. I know him, he would have never hurt you on purpose. His marriage is in a really difficult place right now and to be honest, I'm surprised that he and Sarai are still together. He's been trying for years to do the right thing by his daughter and even she's become a very thin life-line. I really don't think he ever expected to find you. And he damn sure wasn't prepared for you, that's why I tried in vain to keep him away from your ass."

Sarai. Hearing Kyle speak her name out loud made her more than just a female tucked away in another state. Giving breath to her name gave her life. This woman was more than real. *Sarai*...Keenan's wife, the mother of his child. She existed, and trouble or no trouble, she still carried his name and was legally attached to him...still. There was no way my mind could overlook that fact. I wasn't crazy by any means. I had heard all of the stories before from so many different men...they stayed because of the kids, they stayed because of finances, they stayed because of obligations...still...they stayed. For me, as long as you and your wife, girlfriend, baby momma or whoever, were still sharing a life, I wanted no parts of it. I didn't have time for it. That's why I was so angry with Keenan. Unwillingly, I had gone against my own values...he had put me in a situation that made me feel horrible about myself, my feelings, us, everything we shared. I would have never made the choice to sleep with, much less fall in love with, a married man.

"Do you think he loved me?" I asked without really understanding why it was important. Did it matter? The answer wouldn't change the circumstances.

"Yes Toni, I do. I know he loves you. I'm not just saying this because he's my cousin. In fact, I don't want him to. But speaking to him, I know that he has fallen in love with you. Still, I'm going to be completely honest with you just like I was with him. Let this go. Until he's ready to move forward and make a final decision with his marriage, he can't love you…it's that simple. That is a dead end and I can only imagine the wreckage that's waiting at the end. You deserve better. Sarai deserves better."

Her name again. On the lips of my best friend. In my home…occupying my space. How could a woman, who I didn't even know, have this kind of impact on my life?

Of course he was right…Keenan couldn't be in my life anymore…no friendship, no relationship…nothing. I didn't know which would be more difficult to convince, my mind or my body. *Damn.* Back on the horse. I leaned down, resting my head on my knees. I felt Kyle's fingers stroking my hair.

"We'll get through this love. We always do."

Chapter 12: Choices

Two days…maybe three. I sat in the apartment, closed in…shut away from the deafening madness of my life. Closed off from Toni. *Damn.*

There was no one to blame but myself. Why did I think I could love her? I did love her. At some point, during the course of our relationship, I had fallen madly in love with this woman. I had tried desperately to avoid it, yet here I was. Her smell…her taste, left me intoxicated. Our conversations left me yearning. Now I realize why Kyle warned me to stay away. He knew this would happen. He knew I was hovering too close to the flame. I didn't listen and now I've lost her. *Damn.*

My cell phone rang but I didn't want to answer. I had only spoken to Kyle once since Toni and I had our conversation. Since she walked out of my door and out of my life. I just needed time to think…alone, without interference. But the phone was ringing again so unless I answered it, peace would elude me. I reached from the sofa to get it from the coffee table. Sarai. *Daamnn.* Could this day get any worse?

"Yes."

"Really Keenan, I'm getting sick of your shit…I've been calling you for two days…why haven't you answered your phone?" Her voice was high-pitched, either out of anger or frustration. It was difficult to tell at the moment.

"Sarai...I'm sorry. I just have a lot going on right now. I can't...I'm not going to be at your beck and call. What do you need?" I was too tired for this. In my heart, I knew I wasn't being fair. She should not have to deal with the repercussions from my wayward life, but it is what it is. Yes she's still my wife, but I was not kidding myself...our marriage was done. It took Toni to make me realize that. And even though we could not be together...I was not willing to continue with this fraud of a marriage anymore. Not even for my daughter. Amazingly, this recent realization has brought me some semblance of peace. However, I was painfully aware that this peace was going to be jeopardized the very moment I tell Sarai about my decision.

"Look, it's apparent to me that you have decided not to have anything to do with me right now, but I didn't think that you going off on your little hiatus included you being absent from your child. Zy'riah has been asking for you and you won't even have the decency to answer your damn phone. I can't keep going through this Keenan."

There it was...the moment her frustration changed into desperation. The knowledge that I was to blame for her emotions was unsettling. Ashamed, I never once considered that she was calling for Zy'riah. Counting back the days I realized that I hadn't spoken to my baby girl in at least a week. How did that happen? How did I get so consumed with the distractions of my life that I had forgotten to make even the smallest amount of time for her?

All of a sudden, a cloak of weariness enveloped me. I didn't want to fight anymore. At least not tonight.

"I'm sorry Sarai. I really am...I'm just...I just have a lot on my mind right now."

"Whatever you have going on should never interfere with your relationship with our daughter." She stated softly, still angry but noticeably calmer. "You promised me that when you left it wasn't because you were running away from us, but this doesn't feel like it. Give me *something* Keenan. Tell me something to reassure me that we still matter. That *I* still matter. The longer you stay in Atlanta, the further I feel you drifting and it's scaring me. I don't know what I'm supposed to do."

The anger was much easier to deal with than this. This heartbreaking plea. In it, I felt her reaching out to me. Silently begging me for something that I couldn't give. It's not that I don't love her. She is the first love of my life. But I can't say that I'm still in love with her. Not after what I have…*had*…with Toni. I didn't expect to feel what I felt and these emotions have confused the hell out of me.

"Sarai, you're right we can't keep going through this. This situation is clearly not a good one and it's not fair to you, to Zy'riah, not even to me. I think it's time to move forward…we have to end this baby."

I hoped the term of endearment would soften the blow. There was silence on the line and I could only imagine what was going through her mind. This definitely wasn't the plan when I moved from D.C. We were trying to fix this but, the distance only made me realize that we couldn't be fixed. I know this is not what she expected. Hell I wasn't even sure what the expectations were anymore.

"So that's it, you're just giving up on us? You don't want me anymore Keenan?" *Damn.* Tears.

"Be honest with me. I deserve that at least. Tell me her name. Give me the name of the woman that has stolen my husband."

I sighed. No more fights. I thought it was only fair that I gave her what I thought she wanted, the truth. She deserved that. So I told her everything even though I knew each fact, each moment shared would only serve to break her heart even more. *Damn.* When did I become that dude?

"Does she know about me? Does she know about our daughter?"

I explained the entire situation. Although it shouldn't matter, there was a part of me that wanted to protect Toni…to shield her from any of the blame of this irrevocably broken marriage.

"I don't even know what to say Keenan. I just never really thought that we would get to this final point. But you will not leave me to pick up the pieces. You will come home and help me break this news to our daughter. You will help me explain to her how we will not be a family anymore. You owe me that."

I couldn't disagree. I would go home to D.C. and help clean up this mess. I did owe that to them both.

I had some things to tie up in Atlanta before making my trip home. We hung up only after I promised to keep her updated on my plans. The chasm between us wider than ever before.

Chapter 13: Crossroads

For the first time since our ritual began, I didn't feel like going to eat Saturday breakfast with my girls. There was no doubt they would have a thousand questions for me and even though it had been over a week, I didn't feel like answering them. At this point in my process, I just wanted this entire debacle to be forgotten. I wanted, needed to move on. But of course I knew that couldn't happen without first facing my friends and putting my shame and pain on full display. One step at a time.

I did a quick assessment of my appearance in the bathroom mirror. Thankfully, the traces of my ordeal had started disappearing from my face. My crying spells ended about two days ago, so my eyes were no longer swollen or red. The only reminders were the dark circles under my eye, which demonstrated my weariness from not being able to sleep-still. I applied makeup to try and mask the blemishes, bound my hair into a careless ponytail and dressed casually in a light sweater and jeans.

Walking to my car, I noticed how unusually dirty the exterior was. Damn shame the people and things I have neglected over the last couple of weeks. I make a silent vow to get it together. Thankfully, the traffic heading around 285 and 20 was light so I made it to Intermezzo in great time. Dawn and Rae were already there sitting at the bar, waiting for me...waiting to begin their inquisition. Rae noticed me first when I walked in. She quickly jumped off of her barstool to greet me...wrapping me up in a warm embrace. I hugged her back tightly. I have missed my friend and again, I give myself a mental kick for not reaching out to her in my time of need. Next Dawn comes over and gives me a light hug. We head over to our table. When we sit down, we don't even pretend to look at our menus. On this morning, like it or not, ready or not, the hot topic of discussion will be me and Keenan.

The waitress comes over and we hastily gave our orders. The very minute she's out of the line of hearing, Dawn turns to me with a quizzical expression on her face. The inquisition begins.

"Girl, what the hell happened? Are you ok?"

I took a minute to answer the question because, well, there really was no easy answer. Am I ok? Yeah I am. But I am not unscathed. There are new wounds in my heart that only time will heal. I guess recognizing that is the first step in the process.

"Yeah, girl I am. I mean, I will survive, but damn if the blows didn't hurt." I laughed, making a feeble attempt to break the somber mood. It didn't work. I can barely stand the look of pity on Rae's face. Maybe this wasn't such a good idea after all.

Dawn continues. "Dang girl, I can't believe Keenan is married AND has a daughter that he didn't tell you about. What was he thinking?"

I shrugged my shoulders. "That's exactly the problem, Dawn, He wasn't thinking. At least about me anyway."

"I just don't get it. Men can be so selfish," this from Rae, who had finally decided to give her input. "I mean he seemed so perfect but he turned out just like every other dude. So what is he saying? The usual batch of bull?"

I couldn't help but smile a little at the trace of anger in her voice. I expected it. Before I could answer, the waitress returned with our food. I waited until she was again out of hearing range before continuing.

"He's saying that they have been separated for a while, hence the reason he's even in Atlanta. I guess the separation is for both of them to figure out whether or not they are going to try and work it out or if it's really over. I don't know and at this point I really don't care. What I do know is that *I* should have never been a part of the situation."

Rae responded. "Separated does not mean divorced. I don't know what's so difficult to understand about that concept. The whole institution of marriage has been completely redefined in our generation. Either you're married or you're not. Simple as that. If you can't be married anymore...divorce. All of these different story-lines going on just...I don't know...cheapens it all to me."

"I don't know Rae," said Dawn. "You would think I would feel differently having been married, but I'm telling you girl, once you're in it, you realize that it's not all black and white. When Jamie and I first separated, I made a personal vow to not date anyone until we figured out what was going on. I didn't want to complicate my life any more than necessary and I certainly didn't want to make the situation more difficult for Lexie. But you know, there came a point when I became too lonely to keep being alone, yet, I was too afraid to completely let go. Honestly, I can't judge Keenan if he's at that crossroad in his marriage. I've been there and trust me, it's not an easy place to be."

Rae rolled her eyes, "Really Dawn? Are you really going to defend him right now? Unbelievable."

"Hey, I'm not defending him. He still should have told her so she could have made her own decision as to whether or not to get involved with him. I'm just saying you can't just look at his situation out of one-dimensional glasses. That's all I'm saying. Girl love is complicated enough. If they really love each other, maybe somewhere in this mess there is a way for it to be salvaged. I'm just saying."

Again Rae rolled her eyes. "It's not a 'situation'; it's a 'marriage'. You both will do well not to sugarcoat it."

Listening to them both really made me think. Rae's point of view wasn't without merit. In fact, her views were more aligned with my own, or at least where they used to be before I unwillingly distorted them. My own parents had divorced when I was barely a teenager. In my case, my mother left my dad for her high-school sweetheart after reconnecting with him when he moved back into town. This proved to be the downfall of our relationship. My dad and I barely survived those years of turmoil, chaos, and pain. How could I possibly be in the midst of another person's storm, another child's nightmare? It was against everything I knew and love or not, I couldn't face myself in the mirror if I became that woman.

The situation continued to be debated for another hour as we finished our food, ordered and finished coffees and desserts. Even though I had initial reservations about coming out today, I was glad that I decided to come. I needed this. This companionship with the people who love…know me. I needed Dawn's foolishness…needed Rae's rationality. Their realness gave me a sense of sanity.

I checked my watch and realized that it was 2:30 p.m. It would be a good time to head over to Muse. I'm sure Tanya would be glad to have the rest of the day off. I was so grateful for her patience this past week. We said our goodbyes and I headed to my sanctuary away from home.

....

Just as I suspected, Tanya, although thrilled to see me, was much more excited to know that I actually planned on working the rest of the afternoon, meaning she had the rest of the day off. It was obvious that she was curious about what was going on but she respected my privacy and didn't say anything. We are friends, but not close enough for me to give her that kind of personal information. Those conversations were only reserved for Rae and Dawn.

The store was quiet, which granted us the opportunity to engage in gossip that didn't actually didn't include me. I found out that Mia had a new boyfriend, which was good news, although surprising. She hadn't dated anyone since her last serious boyfriend last summer. She said that she wanted to focus all of her time and energy on her final classes needed for graduation. Since this was her last semester, I guess she figured it was time to let her hair down and have a little fun. Good for her. Although I was slightly envious, I couldn't wait to meet her mystery guy. My little Mia was a funny girl and her batch of dates was often an eclectic bunch. To say they were quirky was an understatement. She was a passionate lover of the artsy, moody, self-aware, socially-conscious young brothers, who, I warned, were destined to break her heart. Those were the ones who spouted political rhetoric during the day while whispering poetic words of affections at night. Their intensity could be an all-consuming passion, or it could lead you on a dangerous never-ending emotional roller coaster. You definitely had to be ready for the ride. Who knew that it would be me and not Mia that would end up in this situation now? Life's ironic turns never ceased to amaze me.

After the gossip fest ceased, and Tanya left for home, I fell into my usual routine. Coffee, stocking, inventory. The few people scattered about didn't seem to need much assistance; they either knew what they wanted to purchase or they were simply students, who had come in search of a quiet place to study. Either way, I was glad for the distractions. Glad to be out of the house and like Kyle so eloquently put it, "back to the business of living." The afternoon passed swiftly, and before I knew it, it was almost time to close shop. There was only one person still left in the store, a young man, presumably a college student. Throughout the afternoon, he had been intermittently studying and writing, stopping only to print or reload on coffee. The dark circles under his eyes were evidence of his sleep-deprived condition. Watching him made me reminisce on those hectic, often insane days of mid-terms and final exams. Cramming for tests, inhaling pots of coffee, trying to complete long over-due papers. Every semester, me questioning whether or not it was all worth it. Every semester, Rae and Kyle practically dragging me over the finish line. Then one day, it was over. The chaos, the parties, the exams…it was all behind us. We had become young college graduates full of promise, full of excitement, ecstatic about our chance to put our stamp on the world. Yes…wonderful memories.

The young man began to pack up his belongings and I walked back over to the coffee pot to pour some fresh coffee in a Styrofoam cup with a lid. I was sure that he had a long night ahead of him. I took the cup over to him and extended it. He glanced up and gave me a small, weary smile of thanks before taking it from my hand. I told him good luck and responded with a smile of my own. He finished loading his books, paper, and notes into his book bag, then I walked him to the door, ready to lock up after he left.

Just as we got to the door, I saw the figure of someone about to enter. I was about to let the person know that I was closing early when they walked inside. *Damn.*

Chapter 14: Surrender

I had to see her. Even if she rejected me again. That was a risk I was willing to take. I missed her too much. Needed her too much. Wanted her too much to just let her walk out of my life without me fighting for what we shared. On my way to Muse, I was as nervous as a schoolboy. I checked the time, almost 7 o'clock. I knew I would have to hurry if I was going to catch her before closing. Thankfully, I was now driving Kyle's truck. He offered to loan it to me since he has been using the BMW as his primary vehicle the past weeks. Once again, Kyle to the rescue. Maybe one day I'll have my shit together like him.

He was the one who told me where to find her. They had been together earlier in the week. He said she was broken and when he said it, I could clearly hear not only the anger, but the disappointment in his voice. I had let so many people down. I updated him on my conversation with Sarai, letting him know that I had decided to officially end it. He wasn't really surprised. Kyle had been with us through the ups and was instrumental in getting me through the downs. But he knew that it was not easy for me to walk away from my daughter. It still wouldn't be easy, yet, somehow I had to make it work. I refused to continue living the lie. As much as I didn't want to admit it, Toni was a huge part of my decision. Being with her was like breathing new air. She renewed my soul. I told him I wanted to make it right. He took a long sigh before telling me where she was. Now here I am, on my way to see her, ready to beg for forgiveness.

The Gods, at least, appeared to be on my side. I was able to find parking fairly quickly, not an easy feat downtown.

Rushing to the door, I opened it just as it appeared that she was walking out with some young dude. She stopped dead in her tracks when she saw me. I stopped. It had been a long two weeks since we'd seen or last spoken to each other. She was such a beautiful woman. Nothing about the past weeks had diminished that fact in any way. Her hair was in its usual curly ponytail. She had on a tank top and jeans, looking as if she was one of the numerous college students that peppered the area. No make-up, only lip gloss slickly covering her wide-open mouth. If it wasn't for the young man exiting, I probably would have gathered all of her up right then and kissed and made love to her on the floor. Damn I missed her.

"Hey," I finally said. The young man gave me a look of caution before turning back to face her. She smiled slightly, which, I guess signified that I was safe. He thanked her for coffee then headed out of the door. I moved to the right so that she could lock the door behind him. After flipping her sign to CLOSED and releasing the blinds, she turned around slowly to face me.

"Hey," That was all. Wordlessly she stared…waiting. I could tell from her stance…arms folded defensively, and the look on her face, that she was still angry. Not that I didn't expect her to be, but I had hoped it had dissipated at least a little. This was not going to be easy.

"I need to talk to you. I know that you're closing but give me a few minutes please."

"Why should I do that?" She asked. "What words could you say to me that would change the way I feel?"

I hate this. This coldness…bitterness, coming from someone I know was so far from it. I wanted *my* Toni back. However, I understood that it would take work to get her to trust me again.

"Toni, please don't turn me away. I want you. I need you. You may not want to hear that but I do. I don't think I've ever wanted anyone else as bad. Just let me explain where I am in this journey because I don't want to endure the rest of it without you. *Please*."

Tears formed in her eyes. I felt so much pain and guilt. Who was I to bring her this misery? Who was I to make her life this complicated? Only a man, but a man who was willing to put it all on the line for her. Somehow I had to make her believe that.

She suddenly moved, walking past me to get a cup of coffee. Seeing this was reassurance that I had at least bought some time. Tentatively, I asked for a cup. She didn't respond. I knew she would get it. I went to our normal booth and had a seat, waiting for her to return. She did quickly, handing me my cup before settling in on the other side. I took a sip. A little bit of cream…a whole lotta sugar. Perfect.

"Look Keenan," She started, "I'm going to be very blunt with you. Please don't come in here feeding me a bunch of bull. You have already hurt me more than any man in my life. Why are you here? What do you want from me?"

What did I want? To love her…freely, uninhibited, without boundaries, without issues.

"Listen Toni. I know I don't have the right to even be here, talking to you, asking you for anything. We need to have real conversation about 'us'. I couldn't walk away without you knowing exactly how I feel. Please believe me when I say that I never meant to hurt you. I promise you that I had no intention of falling for you the way that I have, but it happened and I wasn't prepared for that. That's the truth. I should have told you about my wife and child…I just didn't think it would come to that.

This may not make a difference but I had a talk to my wife, Sarai. I told her about you, my feelings, everything. I let her know that our marriage is done. Honestly, it was done before I met you, but…I don't know… matters were complicated with my daughter. I'm ready baby…I'm ready to move on…to have a life with you. I want my life with you in it."

The tears were now streaming down her face. I couldn't decipher them. Couldn't fully comprehend if they were tears of joy or sadness. Of course I hoped it was all for the good. That she was willing to be with me in this crazy, mixed up life.

She spoke softly, "Keenan, how is that supposed to make me feel? Am I supposed to feel good about that? As a woman, how am I supposed to process the news that I may have broken up a home, a marriage. Your daughter…I was that little girl without her parent. How am I supposed to feel about that?"

"You didn't break up my home Toni. I came to Atlanta because my home was already broken. I just didn't know if it could be fixed but being with you confirmed for me that it couldn't. What we had…I haven't had that in a long time and I know that I want it in my life again. I know that I want it with you. Please, baby…give me another chance to make this right. This is too good not to make right."

She sat silently, still crying. I took a chance and moved towards her on the bench. When she didn't move away, I moved in closer to the side of her and enveloped her body in my arms. Gradually, the resistance eased from her body. I was thankful to hold her in my arms again, at least for this moment. I ran my fingers through her soft ball of hair, caressed her neck. The timing couldn't be worse, but I felt my body responding to being close to her. That familiar hint of vanilla teased my senses. I slid the band out of her hair and let it cascade around her face. Strange how in this vulnerable state, she was even sexier. I rubbed my face in her hair. Planted light kisses on her forehead.

Waited. She didn't move. Kisses along her cheekbone. The salt from her tears stinging my lips and tongue. Her breathing changed. She still wanted me just as much as I wanted her.

"Baby…please." My plea not only for another chance but for this opportunity to love her again. I wanted her so badly. My yearning for her threatened to overwhelm me. I grabbed a fistful of her hair and pulled her head back, forcing her to look at me. I could see the apprehension in her eyes and I could understand it. But I didn't want her to be confused about me…about us. I needed to erase any remaining doubts that still existed.

"Keenan, I don't know…I don't know."

I heard her hesitation but I had already decided that I was going to show her what she needed. She needed me loving her. I leaned down and kissed her. I didn't hold back. I wanted her to feel my hunger, my need. I assaulted her mouth, simultaneously sucking and biting her succulent lips. We both moaned as I pulled her into my mouth, our tongues at once finding their familiar rhythm. Her taste filled me, seduced me. I felt her hands in my hair, which only stimulated me more. I abruptly broke away, breathing deeply. I looked into her eyes…dark pools of passion.

"Yes?" I asked. There was a brief pause.

"Yes." She finally surrendered. She let go of my hair and slid out of the booth. She grabbed my hand and led me to the small office in the back. She turned on a desk lamp, emitting a soft glow in the room. I noticed a small sofa in the corner. She offered me a shy smile. I smiled back before closing the gap between us.

I kissed her gently on her mouth. I knew she wanted more but there was too much I needed to give her. I grabbed her tank top with both of my hands, carefully tugging it over her head. I reached around her small back and unhooked her bra, exposing her erect nipples. She whimpered. Damn, it took everything in me to show some restraint. I unzipped her jeans and pulled them down, along with her black laced panties. I gazed up at her quivering, naked body, marveling at her beauty. I was overcome by emotion. Still on my knees, I wrapped my arms around her waist, resting my cheek against her thigh. I felt her fingers in my hair, stroking me, comforting me. This amazing woman, who didn't have to love me after all that I had done, yet, here she was…willing to love me…still.

My hands moved from her waist to her ass, caressing the soft, full mounds. I kissed her thigh…small kisses leading to long licks. Her womanly scent enveloped me…called out to me, begged me to taste her. I spread her legs slightly apart, granting me easier access. Her grip on my hair tightened as she quietly moaned. I kept one arm wrapped tightly around her, steadying her. My other hand I left free to work my magic. I started by taking my thumb and slowly rubbing it over her clit which was slightly peeking from her pink folds. Immediately I felt her juices run down my hand. She was so ready. Her moans grew louder. She called out my name. I removed my hand, not wanting her to cum just yet. But she was too eager.

"Keenan please!" She begged. Her cries were driving me crazy, but I tried to be patient. I gave her more. My tongue found its way to her entrance, lapping at the fountain of honey. She yelled out, pulling me in closer, drenching my face in her wetness. I desperately held on to her body with both arms, trying to prevent her from collapsing to the floor. I licked, sucked, bit…drove her to the edge. But I wasn't ready for her to fall. I pulled away and at that moment, fresh tears lined her face. This time I knew that they were tears of frustration. Relief was coming. Standing, I gathered her petite frame up, and walked to the sofa, spreading her beneath me. I loved the look of passion on her face…loved knowing that I put it there. I wanted to be the only one to put it there. I rushed to remove my clothes. My manhood was swollen and aching from need.

"Look at me Toni." She did. Her face flushed, damp with tears and sweat.

"I love you, do you understand that?" She nodded, while squirming in desperation.

"I need you, do you understand that?"

"Yes Keenan." She breathed.

I grabbed her legs, wrapping one around my waist, the other I carelessly tossed over my shoulder. As I forcefully entered her we both yelled out. *So wet…so warm… so good.*

"I missed you baby." I don't even know whether or not she heard my words, as lost as she was her own haze of ecstasy. I tried in vain to be easy with her, but the feel of her sweaty, hot, squirming body underneath me overwhelmed my senses. Not holding back, I pumped into her, faster, harder. She screamed my name, clawing at my chest, my back. I moaned hers as I pulled her hips to greet me thrust for thrust. My head began to spin as I became lost in the sensations of us…moans, cries, sweat, tears, skin. The reins of my control slipped away until I just couldn't hold on anymore. We climaxed together, collapsing in a tangled, complicated mass of bodies and emotions.

We held on to each other, not speaking. I didn't want to move, fearing that the magical spell of the moment would be broken. I just wanted to stay here, wrapped up in the aftermath of this love, not facing the complications of the reality that was waiting for me.

"Keenan?" My name softly escaping her lips. So much for comfort.

"Yes."

"What do we do now?" *Reality.*

I sat up, unwrapping her legs from around me. Looking at her, I saw the confusion written on her face. Still, even after this, she had doubts. What was it going to take to make this right?

"Now, I tie up some loose ends here before I go back to D.C. Sarai has asked me to come home so that we can talk to our daughter about what's going to happen. I know this will be a process that will take some time, so I'm asking you to be patient with me. I want to be with you, believe in that."

Silence. "I do believe you Keenan. Even though this is against everything that I know, everything that I believe in, I do believe that you love me and you are giving me the truth. But I have to see that you are making progress to end your marriage. This will not be a long-term situation for me. It's already killing me knowing that you still legally belong to someone else."

I leaned down to kiss her fully on the mouth hoping that she could feel how passionate I was in us. She touched my face, kissing me back.

"Make this right."

Chapter 15: Complications

I felt like a fool. I couldn't even help myself. How did I become this person to accept being the other woman? Funny thing is, I didn't feel like the other woman. I felt like THE woman. I thought I would never take him back, but once he walked into Muse, I knew my resolve wouldn't last. I missed him. Beautiful him. That smooth chocolate skin, that body, those lips. I was not prepared to have him back in my space. I was not prepared to have his energy surrounding me. I loved him.

My body betrayed me. I was amazed at how quickly the longing filled me just from being near him. The ache, that had somewhat dimmed over the weeks, returned with a vengeance. I wanted him. Needed him to fill me…claim me. And that he did. Oohhh the things that man could do with his tongue. Just thinking about it now caused my body to flush with heat. How could I let him go?

I was headed to Kyle's. He had invited me over to hang out for the night. I hadn't spoken to him since I had decided to let Keenan back in my life. I knew that our status would be a topic of conversation, as I'm sure he had spoken to Keenan. Either way, I would be glad to see him. We hadn't had a fun night together in a long time. Keenan had wanted me to come over, but I was adamant about not falling back into the pattern of neglecting my friend. I could sense him pouting over the phone but he would be ok…it would be good for him to miss me again.

I pulled up to Kyle's home after about a forty minute drive. The traffic in Atlanta never fails to amaze me at how convoluted it could be. It didn't even seem possible that so many people lived in the city, yet, every day it was the same struggle getting to and from any location. I've read reports that we have some of the worst traffic in the nation. Being in the midst of the madness every day, I could easily believe it. After sluggishly inching my way around a wreck around 285, I was beyond frustrated and grateful to have finally arrived.

Kyle's home is located in Alpharetta, an affluent suburb of Atlanta. Many celebrities for whom Atlanta serve as their home-base, live there. Although Kyle is not a celebrity, his status as one of Atlanta's up and coming young attorneys afforded him the luxury of living in the neighborhood. His home is one of the more modest ones; nevertheless, it is still beautiful. Brick exterior, black shutters, well-manicured lawn. I drove around the circular driveway and parked directly in the front. I called him to let him know that I was outside and in minutes, the door opened. Looking like an Abercrombie and Fitch model, he came bounding down the steps -clean shaven, long bronze legs clothed in khaki shorts, polo shirt. I smiled as I watched him…he was so handsome. He smiled back as he reached out to grab my hastily packed overnight bag.

"Hey love." I greeted him.

"Hey back."

We walked up the steps and into the house. It seemed like forever since I had last visited. My eyes conducted a quick scan, while my brain processed the minor changes. His dining room furniture had been changed. His sitting room had been transformed with new paint. Whereas the room was initially a soft, mint green, it was now a cozy chocolate. The room appeared more inviting bathed in its new hues.

Kyle took my bag to his guest room while I instinctively went into the kitchen. Being the consummate host, he would, undoubtedly, have some snacks prepared and wine chilled in preparation for my arrival. As expected, there was a cheese and fruit tray on the counter along with a bottle of chilled Riesling. I poured two glasses of the Riesling and took them, as well as the fruit and cheese out to chairs on the back patio, my favorite place in the house.

Kyle returned, taking the seat opposite of me. Both of us laid back lounging with our feet on the one long ottoman. It felt really good out here with a slight breeze blowing. The patio overlooked his pool, which appeared freshly cleaned, and his Jacuzzi, both of which I planned on engaging in tonight.

After taking a long swallow of wine Kyle turned to me, smiling that all-American smile.

"So Ms. Toni. What's been good in your life?" He asked with a soft laugh. Oh Kyle. Always the inquisition.

"What do you mean what's good? I'm sure you already have details, what other information are you looking for."

"Oh come on girl. Yeah I've spoken to Keenan but you know I've been waiting to hear from you. Are you really good with the place you guys are in? Seriously, I'm your boy. You know you can tell me your true feelings about all of…this."

"Kyle, baby, I appreciate you, but honestly I'm good. I never would have believed I could be good in a situation like this but yeah, I'm ok. The conversations I've had with Keenan lets me know that he truly loves me and I don't want to lose him. I have to believe him when he says that he's going to make this right and start the divorce proceedings. All I have is his word so until he shows me differently I'm going to stand on it. Even you admitted that he and…his wife *(I could not bring my lips to speak her name)* were having problems long before he met me. That alone assuages some of my guilt."

Kyle sat staring at me as if I was a stranger in his home. I could only imagine what he was thinking. Hearing my own words, I knew I didn't sound like my old self. But I had come to the conclusion that I was not the same woman I had been just three short months ago. This man had changed me somehow, although the verdict was still out as to whether or not it was for better or worse.

"Wow...I have to admit, I never expected you to take that stance. You are always so stubborn, especially when it comes to that heart of yours...I guess it just took the right one."

I thought about his words... it definitely took the right man. I never would have believed that I could be this enraptured by the very essence of a man. My soul connected with him like no man before him. It wasn't just the sex, which is amazing of course, but the way our spirits seem to connect. Nothing just *is* with him...his laughter is like the beat of drums, his words like poetry. What is that? I never even knew this existed in real life. I never saw this chemistry with my parents. Was that the reason that my mother left? Did she go back to the place, the person, where this existed in another lifetime? Life can be so beautiful, yet so complex. So many shades of gray.

"Well friend, as they always say, love changes things. It's certainly given me a different perspective. Anyway...enough about me and my business...what's going on with you?" I asked, pouring another glass of wine.

He shifted uncomfortably. Kyle is such an investigator when it comes to my life, yet he is like an impenetrable safe when it comes to his own personal affairs. Keenan told me that he had gone on quite a few dates with some chick he met in the mall. He had only mentioned her to me once, so I thought she was just another one of his flings. If she's been around for more than three dates, then I should be meeting her. So why is it that he hasn't given me an indication that she is someone to meet?

He still hadn't spoken, choosing instead to also get more wine and nibble on some cheese and crackers.

"Kyle I know you heard me. Isn't there something you need to be telling me? Or more like someone you need to be telling me about. How am I your best friend, yet I don't know that there is some chick that has been around for more than a couple of days?"

He laughed. "I'm going to assume my cousin has told you about Stacy. You know, since you guys are insistent upon having a relationship; we are going to have to establish some boundaries with our lines of communication. I don't need you telling him everything and I damn sure don't need him telling you everything."

Even though I'm sure it wasn't intentional, my feelings were hurt by the tone of his statement. Since when did Kyle become sensitive about me knowing anything about him, especially about any female? In fact, our mutual friends would argue that we share too much information with each other… we've always been that way. Keenan was my first real "secret" relationship, but that's only because of the extenuating circumstances. Now he wants to filter the information I receive. What's really going on with him?

"Really Kyle…so that's where we are now…are you really going to try and monitor the information I get on you? That's so foul and you know it. How am I supposed to feel comfortable sharing my darkest secrets with you when you are not giving me the same consideration?"

He abruptly stood up, taking off his shirt and shorts. In a matter of minutes he was down to his swim trunks. Just like that, in the midst of our conversation, he was going to take a swim. I was familiar with this tactic. He was going to avoid having this conversation. I could literally kill him.

"Stop being so serious girl." He stood there smiling that 1000-watt smile. Even though we were just friends that did not mean that I couldn't appreciate his beauty. His tall body was lean and golden. He was in terrific shape, although I don't know how he managed any time at the gym with his busy schedule. He's always been very specific about his diet. He rarely ate pork and was a king of smoothie recipes, pushing them off on his friends whenever possible. He was led by his ambitions. He believed that he needed exercise and a proper diet to keep his mind sharp. Too bad he wasn't as strict when it came to women.

"This has nothing to do with us as friends…just how I channel information now that we are a group that's all. Anyway, I think this has less to do with our friendship and more to do with your little ass being jealous. Admit it…when you heard about Stacy it killed you to know some other woman may have my heart."

"Your heart? Are you kidding me…damn is it that serious?"

"What? Huh?" Splash. He was in the pool before I could get an answer from him. I couldn't help but laugh. He could seriously work my nerves, but make me love him oh so much.

I went back into the house and hurriedly changed into my bikini. I pulled my hair into a knot on the top of my head and went back out getting into the pool with him. For hours we laughed and played. Leave it to Kyle to bring out the kid in me. We always had so much fun together.

…….

We finally emerged, realizing that we needed to make plans for dinner. I decided to check my phone, sure that Keenan had called. Three missed calls. *Damn.*

Kyle walked into the house to call for takeout so I decided to give Keenan a call back. He answered on the first ring, a sign of his anxiousness.

"Hey."

"Hey yourself." I could easily detect the hint of irritation in his voice. Was he upset that he couldn't reach me?

"Sorry, I just saw the missed calls. We were in the pool. Everything ok?"

"Yes, everything's fine. I was just missing you. I didn't realize that I wouldn't hear from you at all tonight."

"Of course you were going to hear from me babe. As soon as we settled in for the night. I wanted to give Kyle my undivided attention, something he hasn't had in while. You can't be angry, right."

This was something I hadn't counted on. Keenan being jealous of me and Kyle's relationship. Funny, I only thought about Kyle's feelings considering the fact that he was the one losing access to his best friend. I just assumed Keenan would understand. He did know the extent of me and Kyle's relationship before we got involved.

I heard him sigh. I could sense that he was running his hand across his face. I loved that familiarity.

"No Toni, I'm not angry, I'm just…I don't know. Don't worry about it. I'm just glad to hear your voice. I miss you baby."

His tone dropped a few depths when he told me that he missed me. The sexual tension in his voice triggered that oh so familiar ache in the pit of my stomach. Yes, I missed him too.

"I miss you too babe." At that moment Kyle peeked his head out of the door.

"Chinese on the way." He disappeared back inside just as quickly as he first appeared.

"So what time are you leaving tomorrow? I thought we could brunch at Murphy's."

"That sounds great. I'll call you as soon as I wake up. Afterwards, I have to go into Muse because we have a show tomorrow night. Would you like to go?"

I waited anxiously for his answer. Although we've been together now for months, we hadn't progressed to a point of making public appearances at Muse. This definitely would be a huge step for us and would speak volumes to his level of commitment.

"Yes, Toni. I would love to attend the event with you. I'm excited to see the girls again and to meet some of your other friends."

Yes! I could officially say that we were now a couple. Of course I would have to give fair warning to Rae and Dawn of his attendance, so at least Rae would know to be on her best behavior. As expected, she was less than thrilled at me and Keenan's romantic reunion.

"Wonderful. I'm excited too. I will give you a call later on tonight when I get settled in bed ok."

"Only if you promise to read me a naughty bedtime story". At least his wicked sense of humor was back.

"Of course love. I will make it worth your while."

We hung up and I sat thinking for a minute before heading into the house. I really hoped that I wasn't making a mistake. Please Keenan be a man of your word and get this divorce done so that we could go on with the business of living our lives. I know that, regardless of the outcome, he would always have his daughter, so his bond with his wife would not be completely broken. I was willing to deal with that and play my role. I just needed to know that it was final and we were free.

Kyle was sitting on a barstool at the kitchen counter, sipping on what appeared to be his third glass of wine. A new chilled bottle was waiting for me to partake in. When he saw me coming he poured another glass and held it for me.

"Thank you sir."

Across his arm was my favorite blue robe. He opened it as I eagerly slid into the anticipated warmth.

"Oooh yes. This feels so good."

"I know, I know." He laughed as I wrapped the robe tightly around my body and headed to the sofa to relax.

"So what do we have on the playlist tonight? Please don't let it be anything sad, depressing…and no crime dramas."

"Must you always be so demanding; you know, I actually think I'm glad that you have a serious relationship, even if it is with my cousin. You require too much from this man."

He came to the sofa, sitting on the opposite end. I scooted down, pushing my chilled, bare feet under his thigh to absorb his heat.

"I know you don't mean that. No matter who I'm with, you will always be my guy. As a matter of fact, I think Keenan is already a little jealous of the time I'm spending with you. He sounded like it when I spoke to him on the phone. How do you feel about that? Do you think it will cause any problems?"

He was silent for a moment, seeming to process the question. I really wanted to know his point of view. Regardless of me and Keenan's relationship, there is no denying that Kyle would always know him better than I do. He was actually around to witness him grow from boyhood to manhood. Just like there was no denying that he would always know me better, because he knew me first. He was at an incredible vantage point in this trifecta.

He finally spoke…his words in low soft tones. "Honestly Toni, I really don't know how this is going to play out. I love you, but in all fairness to Keenan, I will probably back off a little, as a matter of respect for him as my cousin. If it was anyone else, this wouldn't even be a consideration. You're my best friend and nothing should or will change that. But I don't want my relationship with him to change either. Understand?"

I did. This was another complication that was just going to have to be worked out in due time. Not tonight though. Tonight we were just going to relax and enjoy each other's company.

The doorbell rang. Our food had arrived. Just in time too because all of the swimming and playing had me famished. Kyle went to get the money for the food while I went to answer the door. I was surprised that instead of the delivery guy it was an attractive woman standing on the step.

So this must be Stacy, I thought. I can't believe Kyle had the nerve to invite her over on our night. The intrusion left me livid.

"May I help you?" I asked, refusing to budge from the door to allow her entrance into the home. She looked a little unsure of herself, which made me wonder if Kyle had indeed invited her, or if she had made the unwise decision to show up unannounced. Why is it that he and Dawn always seemed to end up with stalkers? Based on her appearance, she at least seemed classier than his normal females. She wore wide-legged jeans, high-heeled boots, and a button-down crisp white shirt. Her make-up was impeccable and her dark hair was cut in a bob, which hung slightly below her chin. She was definitely an attractive woman.

"Hello," she spoke. "I'm sorry to interrupt. I was looking for Kyle." I noticed her taking in my appearance. I could only imagine what she thought she was interrupting since I was only clad in a bikini and a robe. Surprisingly, she didn't seem angry.

Before I could call for him, I heard Kyle's footsteps coming behind me.

"Toni, I have the money…why are you standing there blocking the door?"

The woman gave a small gasp when she heard my name; I'm sure realizing that I was the "friend" he's spoken of. Instead of answering him I stepped back and open the door wider, revealing his guest.

It is a rare moment when Kyle is speechless. This seemed to be one of those moments. He stood staring at the woman standing boldly on his doorsteps. Then he looked at me with a helpless look on his face. It appeared that he was just as shocked as I was at having an intruder on the night.

"Sarai." The name escaped his lips in barely a whisper. Sarai? Keenan's wife? What the hell was she doing here? I immediately glanced back at the newly identified woman. So that explains the gasp when she heard my name. She had instantly recognized the name of the woman who was her husband's new love. The politeness was gone now that my identity was revealed. She now stood, fiercely glaring at me. I couldn't breathe. Ever since I had discovered Keenan's marital status, I could not bring myself to say her name, to think about her, to actually acknowledge her existence. I didn't want to give life to this person. It made my actions more bearable. Made loving Keenan more bearable, without the guilt, without the pain. Yet, here she was, in Atlanta, invading my home front just as surely as I have invaded hers.

Her countenance warmed as she turned to face Kyle. "Hello Kyle," she started. "I know I'm the last person you expected but I knew that if I called you first you would have talked me out of coming. Sorry to intrude on…this" she casually dismissed me with a small wave of her hand, "but I'm sure you already know why I'm here."

"Well, you have certainly caught me off guard, but come on in." We both moved to the side so that she could enter the premises. It dawned on me that my attire may not be the most appropriate considering the circumstances so I quickly disappeared to the guest room to change into a pair of shorts and t-shirt…leaving Kyle with his cousin's wife. As crazy as I felt, I couldn't begin to imagine the thoughts running through his mind. For a minute, I thought about calling Keenan or at least sending him a text message regarding the new developments. I just as quickly dismissed the idea. This would undoubtedly prove to be a rare occasion to get a feel for the woman who had just presented herself on Kyle's doorstep. I didn't need to ask why she was here. As a woman, I instinctively understood her motivations. She was here to fight for her marriage, to stake her claim on the man she loved. How could I be such a fool? This woman was not going to bow out gracefully as Keenan naively believed.

When I walked back into the living area, Kyle and Sarai were speaking in hushed whispers. Anger and jealousy reared their ugly heads. Yes, Keenan's heart was with me, but legally he was still bound to her. Who was she to try and claim Kyle as an ally? They may have a close relationship as a result of her being Keenan's wife, but Kyle was my best friend, and his allegiance should be with me. Deep within, I knew I was being irrational, but I couldn't help it…my emotions were all over the place. Just a few short moments ago, I was preparing to have a great night and now…my safe haven had suffered this unexpected invasion.

Before I could sit down, the doorbell rang again. This time, it really was the delivery guy. Since Kyle was still deep in conversation, I paid for the food and put it in the kitchen. My appetite had disappeared.

I walked back into the sitting room. Sarai glanced up as I entered. Even though her face was completely blank, her blazing eyes expressed exactly how she felt. I was her enemy. There would be no pretense about that tonight. I walked to the counter and poured my third glass of wine. Probably not the best idea considering the fact that I am usually an inebriated mess even by glass two. But I needed the extra courage to face this woman. Amazingly, even with my nerves wrecked and my head foggy, I still managed to pour the cool liquid smoothly into the glass without spilling it. I took a small sip before I walked over to finally join them.

I felt so sorry for Kyle, who was clearly in a state of distress. I purposely chose not to sit next to them on the sofa, deciding instead to sit on the opposing loveseat. I pulled my legs under me and pulled my wet hair out of its restricting band, allowing it to fall wildly around my head. Waited.

"You *are* beautiful." Shockingly, her voice lacked the intensity displayed in her eyes. I didn't expect this. This quiet tone of resignation. I did not reply, just silently waited for the flow of other words that I'm sure were coming. I didn't have to wait long.

"Well I can certainly say that this wasn't the welcome I had anticipated." A small laugh. One that didn't register much humor. "So you are *Ms. Toni*. The woman who has somehow managed to sneak her way in and steal my husband's heart. I'd hope to meet you but not under these circumstances."

"Yeah well I guess at some point we were going to meet. I just envisioned it being on your grounds, not *mine.*" Hopefully she could detect just how aggravated I was that she would bring this battle to my home field. This situation was turning out to be a disaster.

A flash of anger in her eyes, nevertheless, she remained calm.

Kyle obviously sensed the tension between us. He looked from her to me and back to her. Being the mediator, he stepped in before the situation could escalate further than it had.

"Look ladies. Obviously this is a difficult situation for everyone. Hell I'm not even in it and it's almost more than I can handle. Sarai why don't I get you settled in and maybe we can figure all of this out in the morning."

We both looked at him as if he had lost his mind. Did he really think that we could stay in the same house? I didn't want her here. As far as I was concerned, she could drive to the nearest hotel. Her convenience was not my concern. Before I could express my growing irritation at the open invite, Sarai spoke up.

"So she's staying here? Why is she here with you and not with Keenan?" There was a hint of accusation in her voice.

"Sarai, Toni is my best friend. We were actually having a friendly sleepover before you unceremoniously appeared at my door. I'm just trying to make the most out of this situation."

"Your best friend? Kyle please don't tell me that you had anything to do with this?" She pleaded, "Tell me that you didn't have anything to do with my husband leaving me." Her pretty face was marred with pain. Kyle let out a long sigh and looked at me. I could hear his unspoken words. These were the circumstances he had tried desperately to avoid. I had been so consumed with my own feelings that I had dismissed his concerns. Now the consequences of my selfish behavior were manifesting themselves his reality. My friend had unwillingly gotten caught up in our web of trouble.

"No Sarai, I only introduced them."

"Sarai please don't blame Kyle." There, I had spoken her name aloud. Might as well, the imaginary wall had disappeared. "Blame us, blame me and Keenan. Hell blame Keenan, because honestly I didn't even know you existed when we first got together."

"But you know *now*. And still you are here."

"Yes. I am here, even though a few short months ago I could almost guarantee you that I wouldn't be the woman that would still be here. But I *love* him. I'm not trying to hurt you. Really I'm not. But I've fallen so hard for this man, and he has vowed to me that he loves me too. I believe him and I believe it when he told me that his marriage, your marriage was done."

"*Done?* See that's exactly the point, as far as I was concerned we were working on our marriage. It was not *done* as you so casually put it. I was not trying to be *done* with my marriage after nine years. I was not trying to be *done* with the man who is the father of my child. *You* are the reason Keenan says he is done. If he would have never met you then I can't see

that he would have walked away from me…from our baby."
Up until this moment, she had managed to contain her
composure, but her emotions overpowered her. Tears poured
down her face as her hurt and anger exploded. I wanted to
escape. This was too much to deal with, especially in my
inebriated state. Looking at Kyle, I knew that right here, in this
moment, is the last place he wanted to be. We looked at each
other, helpless to get beyond the moment. I rubbed my temples,
feeling the pangs of an oncoming headache.

Kyle finally spoke. "Sarai, sweetheart I know you're
hurting but I think the person you need to speak with is
Keenan. Toni is involved, but at the end of the day, Keenan
ultimately has made the decision to leave. Even without Toni, I
know you guys were struggling. You guys just need to figure out
where to go from here, because there's a little girl that doesn't
deserve all of this."

"Does Keenan even know that you're here?" I couldn't
resist asking even though the timing couldn't possibly be worse.

"No, for the same reason that I didn't call Kyle, I didn't
want to give him the opportunity to talk me out of it. I left
Zy'riah with my parents so that we could spend some quality
time together. I think that if he just sees me…be in my
presence, without the stress, maybe he will remember some of
the good times and not just the bad. He may think he loves you
Toni, but I promise you, whatever he has felt for you in these
last few months does not compare to what that man has in his
heart for me in our years together. Believe that."

With that bold statement, she abruptly stood up. She
looked back at Kyle. "Kyle can I please get settled in a room. It
has been a long trip and an even longer night." She then looked
both of us in the eye. "I would appreciate it if neither of you
called Keenan. I plan on calling him in the morning before
going to see him and, Toni, I would hope that you will respect
the fact that I need to speak to him alone."

I just looked away. She was making a lot of demands for someone who made the rash decision to interrupt my life. But I guess between the two of us, she still legally had that right.

Kyle got up from the sofa and led her down the hall to his office, which also had a futon. Tomorrow she probably would get the room that I am now in, since that was his main guest room. The irony was not lost on me that somehow we would once again end up as strangers forced to share the same bed.

I watched Kyle stroll slowly back up the hallway. I could tell from the expression on his face that he was distressed. As soon as he sat down I asked him if he wanted me to go.

"Toni, I don't know what needs to happen anymore. This thing has turned into such a mess and somehow it has become my mess, which I really don't appreciate." His weariness was evident.

"Did she say how long she was staying?"

"I don't think she knows. She took two weeks of vacation from her job so I would say at least that long. Or, until she convinces Keenan to give their marriage another try. Whichever comes first."

"Kyle, do you think there's a chance of her convincing him? He loves me right?" I knew I sounded anxious but the implications of Sarai's visit were not lost on me. He could leave me and go back home. That was my reality.

He looked at me. "Honestly Toni, like I just told Sarai, the only person with all of the answers is Keenan. I know that he loves you. I know that there were problems before you were in the picture. But…I also know how much he loves that little girl. And if he thinks Sarai is going to interfere with his time with her, because of her anger, he may stay. Or at least give it another try. Again…I don't know."

"I'm going to leave and head home. Are you going to call Keenan? I don't think it's my place to call him."

"You don't have to go…stay, at least until the morning. You have been drinking. And yeah, I will probably call Keenan, against Sarai's request. He's my cousin, my brother. I won't let him be blindsided. That's just not fair and if it was me, I have no doubt that he would let me know what's up."

I thought about it for minute before finally giving in and deciding to stay. I shouldn't be driving and even if I was sober, I definitely wasn't in the right state of mind to concentrate on the road or other drivers. I would stay, and as difficult as I knew it would be, I wouldn't answer Keenan's calls. This situation was nothing that could be discussed over the phone or texts. I would let him meet with Sarai, then he and I would talk, face to face. I needed to look him in the eyes and know that his love for me was still strong. That he, wanting to be with me was still what he wanted to do, no doubts. Damn, how did I get myself in this?

I went over to the couch, stretched out, lay my head in Kyle's lap. He began stroking my hair, allowing another long sigh to escape.

"What a fine mess you have us in girl."

A fine mess indeed.

Chapter 16: Nine Years

Silence. That's about all I could give Kyle after he called me tonight to give me the heads-up that Sarai was in Atlanta and staying at his house. Why the hell was she here? So fucked up. I came here to get peace, she has decided to bring the battle to me. What exactly was she expecting? I wanted to call her, but Kyle thought it was best if I waited for her to call me in the morning. In the meantime, I prepared for a sleepless night. Way too many thoughts were running rampant in my head.

I sensed something was wrong, but I never imagined this. Several times, I had attempted to contact Toni, but she wasn't answering her phone. Now I know why. What was she thinking? I know she was upset about these circumstances and I don't blame her. I never meant to create all of this drama for her or for Kyle. Maybe I should have allowed her to walk away. I could have gotten a divorce, and then tried to work things out with her. But I couldn't stay away from her for that long. And now that selfishness has put all of us in the middle of an emotional tidal wave.

I walked into the kitchen and got a beer from the fridge. Thinking back to the night before, I had to laugh at myself. For a minute, when Toni was not answering her phone, I was afraid…and jealous. Not for the first time. I wondered if something could be going on with her and Kyle. I didn't think either one of them would betray me, but I had to admit that their relationship, their closeness, left me enviable. She loves Kyle. Of course what she feels for him pales in comparison to her feelings for me. Still, it's not easy for me knowing that they had pieces of each other's heart. Cousin or not, brother or not, that revelation was not easy to digest.

Restless. I walked back into my sitting room and decided to play some music. Jazz would work well tonight in my state of desolation. *Sarai.* Thinking of her made me reminisce on our love story. Back then, she was the cute girl from around the way. We had mutual friends but were never that close until we both ended up at Howard. Even though I was a local, I still opted to stay on campus. I wanted to get a feel for adult life without the rules and restrictions of home. At the time, I thought me and Kyle would attend college together, creating a memorable journey. Until Kyle surprised everyone when he announced that he would be going to college at Georgia State University. I was in disbelief. I couldn't understand why he was leaving me behind. To go to Georgia? I didn't care that it was Atlanta, it was still the south, which I considered to be foreign territory. Either way it was far away and for the first time I wouldn't have my best friend with me.

Living on campus proved to be exciting, but daunting. It was difficult having to meet new people and build new relationships. That first day on the yard, Sarai and I saw each other, and clung to each other for dear life. Later, we discovered other friends, but we still remained close. At some point she caught feelings for me, I can't remember when or how. One night, after a step-show, we found ourselves alone in my room, kissing, touching… making out. The sex good…really good in that young love kind of way. Our exploration was exhilarating. At first, I rebelled against a relationship. I wanted to keep my freedom, especially with all of the hot and eager girls on campus. It was pointless. Sarai was always there and somehow what we had evolved into something.

After graduation she got the job at the marketing firm. Once she became established in her role, she used her connections to get me hired. Our relationship continued. She was my friend and my lover. She was caring, gentle, kind. A good woman who I was blessed to have.

After obtaining our degrees and finding jobs, it seemed the next logical step was to get married. So we did just that. Our finances were limited so we had a small ceremony at her church with minimal family and friends present. From that point, our American dream began. We settled into our jobs, started making good money and even managed to buy a small house near my parent's neighborhood. Gradually, we climbed the social ladder, engaging in D.C's lively nightlife, participating in corporate events like company barbeques and picnics. We decided not to have children right away, as our jobs kept us busy. Then, four years in…Zy'riah arrived. I thought I knew the definition of love, but there was no emotion that could compare to the feelings I had when I held my baby girl in my arms for the very first time. Even fresh out of the womb, she was the most beautiful sight. In that moment, I knew I would always protect her, always love her…be willing to lay down my life for hers. And I felt the same way now. There was nothing I wouldn't do for her. She was my life. Well almost nothing. Even my love for her couldn't keep me and Sarai together.

Looking back I couldn't pinpoint the moment when our relationship changed. Even before Zy'riah, tensions developed. Our life together was definitely a good one, but there always seemed to be something missing. Something in me that wasn't fulfilled. Partly to blame was my lack of ambition for the job. While Sarai excelled, eventually moving into a management position, I just didn't seem to have the same level of commitment. The mundane routine of the nine to five was killing me spiritually. I began to hate the suits, the never-ending meetings, the corporate functions, the backstabbing…the facade. At heart, I was an artist. I loved painting, drawing, writing…anything that allowed me to creatively flow. Unfortunately, I always knew that it would be unacceptable to Sarai and, of course, my parents for me to spend my days struggling and starving until I could gain recognition for my work. Sarai once succinctly told me that there was a significant difference between a hobby and a career, clearly implying that painting should be in the former category. Armed with that knowledge, I relinquished my dream for corporate America. Still, there came a point where I felt that I was suffocating and my survival instincts would not allow my spirit to die. Against Sarai's wishes, I stocked up on supplies and spent all of my free time creating pieces that had been held hostage in my head.

A friend of mine, a coffee shop owner, allowed me to showcase some of my work. We held a small reception and actually got some of the pieces sold for decent prices. I took the money from the sales, put it in savings and quit. That was the beginning of the end. In Sarai's mind, I was failing our family. In my mind, I was saving myself. Besides, how could I ever teach my daughter to chase her dreams if I wasn't willing to make sacrifices for my own?

Life suddenly became more complicated and we stopped talking. Zy'riah became our one thing in common. I stopped going to functions with Sarai. Partly because I wanted to be done with that world, but it was also because it was evident that Sarai was uncomfortable and somewhat embarrassed of her once successful husband who threw his career away to become a bum. We drifted and try as we might, we could not find our way back. Hence, the separation and pending divorce.

Now, she was here and from my conversation with Kyle, I could only determine that she was here to fight for us. Or at least what we once were. Why was I foolish enough to believe that she wouldn't try and fight, especially after I told her about Toni? Did she really want me? Or was it that competitive nature that made her so successful? Hopefully, by tomorrow morning, I would have some answers.

....

There was no phone call. Instead, promptly at 8 a.m., the doorbell rang. I could only guess that it was her. I was still on the sofa, where I eventually fell into a restless sleep. Walking to the door, I felt as if I was about to open Pandora's Box. When I opened it, she stood there looking apprehensive. It was great seeing her. I hadn't seen her in months and I had almost forgotten how pretty she was. She was dressed down in jeans and sneakers with a long-sleeved t-shirt. Her hair was pulled back into a bun...makeup simple, eye shadow and lip-gloss. I had gotten so used to her in business attire that it was strange seeing her in this state. She looked more like that young, fun girl I fell in love with so long ago. Without saying a word, I stepped back to allow her to enter.

We stood for a moment watching each other. Without warning tears glistened in her eyes. I wanted to be so angry with her for this rash intrusion, but seeing her like this, vulnerable and weak, broke down my defenses. I pulled her into my arms, where she collapsed into an emotional mess. It was a while before she was able to calm down and speak. She pulled away...gazing up at me.

"Keenan, I'm sorry for just showing up like this. I didn't know what else to do. I realized after we spoke that I can't lose you. My family means too much to me...you mean too much to me...for me to just let it go without a fight. I thought, maybe, if I came here, if we just spent some time together me and you, we can remember what we used to be. Please, give us that chance."

This was hell. Talking to her on the phone was one thing...having her here in person...having to personally witness the evidence of her pain, was completely different. I was unprepared for this.

I gestured towards the sofa. "Sit down for a minute. Let me get myself together so we can have a real conversation. I need to get some coffee...have you eaten?"

She shook her head no as she walked over to the sofa. I went into the kitchen to get some coffee brewing. I checked the fridge and pulled out bacon and eggs, something I could make really quickly. Sarai stood, observing the surroundings.

"You know," she spoke, "It's a little strange being in a space that's yours only. Kind of reminds me of visiting you in your dorm."

"Yeah well it's not much, but I've tried to do my best with it. You know I'm not really much for decorating. That was always your forte."

Small laugh. "Yeah I do know. It's nice though…it feels like you."

I didn't comment, just continued to prepare the bacon, eggs, and toast. It did feel strange, especially for me, to have her in this space. So many moments shared with Toni in that very room. I never imagined that Sarai would ever be here.

I announced that the food was ready so she moved to the bar from her spot on the sofa. I arranged the food on two plates and prepared two cups of coffee, one black, one with a little cream and a whole lotta sugar. I passed a plate to her along with the cup of black coffee then came around to sit next to her at the bar.

"Thanks so much for the food and especially the coffee. I'm actually starving since I didn't have time to eat. When Kyle told me that he called you, I figured I needed to get over here as soon as possible."

"Don't worry about it." I stated between my own mouthfuls of eggs. I didn't eat much last night so I was also starving.

"You know…I have to admit that I do miss you cooking for me. You've always been better at navigating around the kitchen than I ever was."

Memories. Being an only child of working parents, I learned how to take care of myself at a young age. At some point, Kyle and I grew tired of always eating hotdogs and Ramen noodles so we began experimenting with different foods. Sarai, on the other hand, is the baby of four kids, so she has always been spoiled rotten. Her domestic skills leave much to be desired. I never minded though. We enjoyed the roles we played.

We finished the rest of our meal in silence. I grabbed the dishes and loaded them into the dishwater, while Sarai went back to her spot on the sofa. I purposely chose not to sit by her. I wanted to talk to her face to face, to make sure that our line of communication was clear.

Feeling no need to beat around the bush, I spoke first. "Sarai, tell me why it is that you have traveled all of this way to see me. Tell me exactly what it is that you are looking for."

"It's simple. Initially after our talk, I was resigned to the fact that we would divorce and I would just have to find a way to pick up the pieces for me and Zy'riah. Then, I spoke to my mom and she brought me back to my senses. She said that no woman allows another woman to take what's hers without a fight. So I'm here, fighting for you…fighting for our family. I love you, you can't doubt that."

I didn't doubt it. And of course I still loved her too, we've had nine years of marriage together…but it wasn't the same.

"Sarai, we've talked about this on numerous occasions. Our problems didn't just appear overnight. We've been struggling for a while. We are not the same two kids shacking up in the dorm rooms. We are not the same two people who shared the same dreams and goals. I love you...but what we had, it's over."

I needed for her to understand that I wasn't just speaking words so the entire time I spoke, I made sure to look directly into her eyes. I could see the tears beginning to form again, but this time I wouldn't be moved. Suddenly, she was beside me. Without warning, she grabbed my hands in her face.

"Keenan you don't mean that. I know the only reason you're even thinking like this is because of what you think you have with Toni. But baby I love you...I need you. Tell me what you need. We can make this right. I've missed you so much."

She started stroking my face and surprisingly my body betrayed me by responding to her touch. She leaned in to kiss my neck, my jaw-line, my forehead...*Damn*. Her kisses felt good...too good. Soft...sweet. I grabbed her hands. I had to stop this before it could get out of hand.

"Sarai...don't...the last thing we need to do is complicate matters."

"Keenan, you are still my husband. I still want you. Be with me and remember...remember how good it can be."

I let go of her hands and stood up, walking to the window.

"I've never forgotten how could it could be. The problem is, I also can't forget the bad times, and those unfortunately, outweigh the good ones in the end. I wouldn't know how to begin to rekindle something that was lost so long ago."

"That's why I'm here now. Let's take this time and see if we can get the good times back. I can't let us go without at least knowing that we did everything we could to save us. I'll be willing to do whatever it takes. You want to do art, do art. You want to go to counseling, we'll do that. We owe it to ourselves and our daughter not waive that white flag so easily."

I turned to her, I'm sure, looking just as confused as I was feeling.

"Why now Sarai? You haven't been willing to give me 100% in months, and now you come here ready to jump in the ring like Ali. I can't help thinking that the only reason you're here now is because of my relationship with Toni. I'm not sure that I'm willing to sacrifice what I've found with her, only to realize you just wanted to win."

She looked stunned and hurt by my words. I didn't care. There was too much at stake, too much to lose.

"I can't believe that you would think that. Toni is *not* the reason I'm fighting. I'm fighting because I love you. Why is that so hard for you to understand? I've never stopped loving you. I just assumed you needed space to get your head together. Never did I think you would actually go and find someone to replace me. That hurt. Yes I was willing to walk away because I was tired of fighting for someone who didn't want to fight for me. I'm not willing to walk away anymore Keenan. I've given too much to this relationship, this marriage. If you can't see or understand that, then I don't know…maybe we have drifted too far apart to make this right again."

She moved from the sofa and came to where I was standing by the window. Her arms encircled my waist. She pressed her face against my back. I couldn't fight her.

"Don't let it be too late Keenan. Give me some time. We can fix this baby."

Damn. Why did she have to come here? I was so ready to move forward. So ready to begin my new life with Toni. Her pleas were easing their way into my conscious. Maybe I did owe us more time…at least for my daughter's sake. How is it that even with the best of intentions, I have managed to complicate my life?

I turned towards Sarai. The hope in her eyes made my heart ache. I couldn't make any promises for the future, but for now this woman standing before me was still my wife. She deserved better. I kissed her softly on the forehead.

"Maybe."

Chapter 17: All Good Things

Why hadn't he called? I looked at the clock. Only twenty minutes had passed since the last time I glanced at it. This was driving me insane.

I needed coffee. Maybe I should be making tea to calm my nerves. Muse has a big showcase tonight so I should be preparing for the long night ahead, but I couldn't rest. My mind was too crowded with thoughts.

It was almost 2'oclock. I had left Kyle's at 5 a.m., not wanting to face him or Sarai. I didn't know what to expect. I prayed that she would meet with Keenan and he could explain to her face to face how much he loves me and wants to be with me. Prayed that she would be on the earliest flight out of the city. But now…now it was getting late and I didn't know what to think. Didn't he know that I would be waiting for him to call? Didn't he care? There was no way that I was going to call Kyle to see if he knew anything. After our disastrous night, he could benefit from a little space. So I'm not going to call him. Or Keenan. When he was ready, he would find me.

Deciding on tea, I put water on to boil, then went to pick my outfit for tonight. Tonight was special. Muse was hosting a showcase for young talent. We had about ten artists scheduled to perform. The tickets were pre-sold and the event was sold out less than a week of them going on sale. At Daniel's suggestion, the proceeds from the event would be distributed among various charities around Atlanta. With a packed house, we were betting that we would profit mostly from alcohol sales.

I was more than excited about the event. We were getting a lot of much needed publicity. A representative from the Atlanta Journal Constitution would be present, as well as a representative from Atlanta Life, a popular social magazine. Mia and I would be co-hosting the event, while Daniel and Tanya would concentrate on working the floor.

Rae and Dawn would be there. Kyle was also scheduled to come. At least before last night. I really hoped that he still decided to come. It seemed that a Who's Who list of socialites would be in attendance and he, being an up and coming attorney, could certainly benefit from being on the scene.

I was just as uncertain about Keenan. Although he had agreed to come, these new developments could hinder that plan. This would have been our first major event together as a couple.

Probing through my closet, I came across a silver, off the shoulder dress that I hadn't worn in minute. It would be perfect for the occasion. I quickly scanned my collection of accessories and chose the ones that I felt were best suited. Tonight, I would wear my hair loose. Even though my confidence was waning by the minute, I didn't see the need to let everyone else know that my world was falling apart.

The shrill piercing of the teapot interrupted my thoughts. I carefully laid the dress across the bed and went back into the kitchen. 2:15 p.m. This is ridiculous. What could he possibly be thinking at this moment? The mere fact that he didn't immediately call me after talking to Sarai caused my heart to sink. He was going back. Maybe I was being paranoid, but I couldn't shake the ominous feeling in my gut. Somehow, she had convinced him to try and save their marriage. Why was I a fool to think otherwise? Separated, not divorced. Big difference. He no more belonged to me at this point in our relationship than he had on the first night we met. The harshness of that realization was finally hitting home. The reality is that I may not ever be free to love him completely. When I walked away the first time, I should have really let him go. I would have, if I would have been thinking with my mind instead of my heart. Kyle was right. This was a no-win situation from the beginning and I should have been cautious of the pending heartache.

There was nothing to be done about it now. In a few short hours I would be co-hosting one of our biggest events. Time to put my game face on for the public, presenting the façade of a business woman who had it all together…meanwhile my heart was shattering in a million pieces.

....

As I drove around to the back of Muse, I noticed, with pride, that the parking lot was already more than half full. Even though the show wasn't scheduled to start until 7:00 p.m., many of the wise ones knew to come early enough in order to get a seat near the stage, if at all. At times like this, I wished we had a bigger spot. There have been occasions when people have been turned away at the door due to the fire code. I always hated to do it. Daniel had been looking into larger spaces that were also cheaper. The problem: even though the rent is pretty steep for this area and the venue is small, this is a prime location, which makes staying here a more viable option, at least for the time being.

I took a swift glance of the parking lot to find Kyle's BMW. I wanted to call him. Tonight was a huge night for me, for Muse. More than ever I needed his support…especially not knowing whether or not Keenan was going to bother showing up. It was difficult to tell in the sea of cars. I did notice Rae's gold Camry already occupying a space. I was glad that she was here early. There was so much to fill her in on. I had yet to tell her about Sarai being in town. I just didn't have the strength to deal with it today in my already anxious state.

Hastily, I walked to the door. Although it's usually humid at this time of night, there was a chill in the air. I hadn't grabbed my sweater when I walked out of the house so I was unexpectedly cold. At least I was sexy.

....

Mia was the first person I spotted as I walked in. She ran to hug me, her face flushed with excitement.

"Toni! Look at the crowd. Isn't this amazing?" She exclaimed. Standing near the front, I took notice of the room around me. Daniel made an executive decision to hire an event planner for the occasion, since Tanya nor myself had much time lately. Both of us, being consummate control freaks, found it difficult to relinquish that power, but we eventually came around, realizing it was for the best. The place was decorated beautifully. The table settings were completed in tones of chocolate and red, which complimented Muse's warm golden walls. The lights were dimmed and there were candles and orchids on every table, adding to the romantic ambience. People were congregating, drinking, taking photos, chatting, networking...the usual fare for Atlanta events. I could tell from their expressions, that everyone was already having a wonderful time. I was proud.

"Yes Mia...this is absolutely amazing."

"You wouldn't believe how busy we've been already. The cash bar has been booming. Oh and before you disappear to your hosting duties, Daniel has been looking for you. Some of his partners purchased a table and I think he wants you to greet them. You know how they are," she stated rolling her eyes, "They always feel like they are entitled to VIP treatment just because of their relationship with him. I swear the people in this city always believe they are way more important than they really are."

I laughed at her frustration. Sometimes I think that Mia is so much like me that we actually could be sisters.

"Well he's going to have to wait a little longer. Have you seen Rae? I saw her car in the lot, but I haven't spotted her since I came in."

Mia took a look around. "Yeah, I put her and Kyle at a table close to the front, I see Kyle still at the table, but no signs of Rae. She probably just went to the restroom. I'm headed that way so if I see her I will promptly send her your way. See you in a little while."

With that she disappeared. I looked towards the front of the stage and sure enough there was Kyle. Smiling, I made my way over to where he was sitting. It thrilled me to know that he was here to support me even with all of the drama that occurred last night. Seriously, I wouldn't blame him if he chose not to speak to me for a minute. But not my Kyle, who has always been there with me through my most difficult circumstances. I don't know why my expectations would have been any differently in this situation. Tonight, he looked even more handsome in a vest and button-down peach shirt. I wouldn't normally approve of that color on a man, but against his bronze skin it looked incredible. He was looking at his phone, his long legs stretched in front of him. I quietly slipped into the empty chair beside him and lay my head on his shoulder. He smiled without having to look up.

"Hey love." He simply stated.

"Hey back," I responded, "I'm glad you came."

"Did you think that I wouldn't?" He asked, turning to face me…his eyes wide with surprise.

"Honestly, I didn't know, Kyle. One of these days you may actually decide to walk away from me and all of the foolishness going on in my life. And I can't say that I would blame you. I really am sorry about last night…hell, I am really sorry about the last few months. You didn't ask for this intrusion."

He stared at me for a minute without saying anything. For the first time, I looked away, feeling slightly uncomfortable under his scrutiny. He reached up to stroke my curls…his finger lightly traced my jawline.

"If you never believe anything else lady, know this…I would never walk away from you. I would never leave you. You mean too much to me for me to ever hurt you that way."

I blushed, hearing his profession of emotions. Somewhere in the back of my mind, I heard Dawn's previous warning. I tried to push it back.

"Thank-you, babe." Trying to lighten the mood, I joked. "You know I always say I'm a work in progress, so continue to be patient with me in this progression."

He laughed too and a wave of relief washed over my body. Losing Kyle was something that I could not afford to do. My sanity would be in jeopardy.

"That you are girl…but then again…so are we all."

Before I could ask him about Rae's whereabouts I heard Daniel's familiar booming voice behind me.

"Toni! I've been looking for you…I have some people I want you to meet. What's up Kyle? Sorry to interrupt."

Looking in Kyle's direction, I rolled my eyes, out of Daniel's sight. He smiled that gorgeous smile.

"Yes Daniel, I know. I was just coming to find you." I quickly lied. I leaned over and kissed Kyle on the cheek.

"I'll talk to you later. When Rae comes back tell her to find me. *Please.*" I purposely stressed so he would understand how desperately I wanted to be rescued. As I stood to follow Daniel, my eyes of their own accord, turned towards the door, pulled by an unseen force. I felt his presence before I even saw him. *Keenan.* Our eyes locked across the room. *He came.*

A brief wave and a small smile. I waved back. Damn, he looks good. His locks were pulled back into his usual ponytail and he looked as if his goatee was freshly trimmed. A crisp white shirt accentuated his physique and his mahogany skin tone. His black jeans were molded to his thighs. I wanted to sprint from Daniel's side and run to him but, I held my composure. Although I was thrilled to see him, it didn't change the fact that he never called. And that fact has left me unsure of where we stand. But he came, and I am glad.

I turned back to look at Kyle. He was watching me. I tried to hide my angst, but he knows me all too well.

This won't be fixed at the moment, so I put my game face back on and follow Daniel through the growing crowd- away from Keenan.

....

She was the first face that I saw when I walked into Muse. As usual, she was a stunning sight. Her hair was a curly halo surrounding her pretty face…her off the shoulder silver dress clung to her body perfectly. Her thighs and ass were perfectly accentuated. My heart ached at the sight of her. How could I be so madly in love with this woman…yet still contemplate giving my marriage another chance? Even if I gave Sarai, my marriage, the benefit of the doubt, could I ever really walk away from Toni? My soul is at ease whenever she's around and that's something I've never experienced before. That's a blessed feeling I could not take for granted. The burden of my choice was weighing me down.

I headed towards Kyle at a table near the front. I hadn't spoken to him since last night and I was anxious to see him, to make sure that we were ok. I felt horrible. I'm sure he never imagined that having me here would cause him so much drama. He stood up as I got closer. We shook hands, before I leaned in giving him a brotherly hug.

"What's up man?"

"What's up with you player?" His eyes were smiling so I knew he was joking.

"Man this has been one hell of a day, but I'm sure you know that already."

"Of course," He replied, "Right now I wouldn't trade places with you for all of the money in the world. Your shit is falling apart man. Ironic how I'm known as the player, but you're the one who's got females all twisted, flying hundreds of miles to find your ass."

The irony of the situation was not lost on me. Being with Sarai took me off of the market early so for most of my life, I've worn the titles of boyfriend, husband…father. Not "player." Mostly, I watched from the sidelines as Kyle actually played the game. Sometimes I was jealous of his freedom, but for the most part I was content.

I never thought that I would be in this situation…deciding which of two absolutely wonderful women to share my life. I had to figure out a solution and fast before it got even more complex than it was already.

Kyle left to get drinks. While he was gone, Rae appeared looking stunning in a black one-piece pantsuit. Her short hair was striking with its recently added blonde highlights. She greeted me a warm hug…leaving me to guess that she had not spoken with Toni yet. In the few short months that I have come to know her, I've learned that she is very protective of her best friend. Honestly, she probably would have been ready to curse and fight me tonight if she had spoken to Toni about the recent developments. I didn't think she would ever speak to me again after finding out I was married, but I made promises that I was moving forward. Now, I've taken three steps back.

"Hey Keenan…I haven't seen you in a minute. How are things going? I would probably know myself if you ever let my bestie come up for air once in a while."

I couldn't help but laugh. For such a small person, she had a tremendous personality.

"I'm good Rae. And stop putting all of the blame on me. I think Kyle gets as much time as I do. Hell sometimes I feel like I have to fight to get her attention."

Rae rolled her eyes. "I can believe that. I have to constantly remind them that she does have another best friend, who, mind you, was actually her friend first, not that that small fact makes any difference. Where are they anyway? I think the show's about to start and I haven't even seen Toni. Let me guess, did I lose Kyle to some chick?"

I let her know that Toni was being held hostage by Daniel and Kyle went to get drinks. I caught his attention at the bar so he would know to bring one back for her as well. We made small talk while we waited for Kyle…not an easy task since music was now playing and the place was more occupied than previously. I was curious as to Dawn's absence, but she told me that Lexie had suddenly become ill. I was sorry to hear that. Dawn and I really connected. Being from Detroit, she had that street edge that I was used to in women. Kyle returned with drinks just as Mia took the stage. Immediately, there was loud applause. Out of the corner of my eye, I saw Toni amble to the side of the stage, ready to take over her hosting duties. She looked in my direction. I offered her a small nod. I could tell she was nervous, but I knew she would be fine. This was her night to shine. After Mia's introduction, Toni took the mic, also to loud applause. As excited as I was about the show, I couldn't wait for it to end, to get her alone in my space. She was radiant in her element.

The show, itself, was a blur of young artists singing, rapping and reciting. It was refreshing to see young kids following and fighting for their dreams. The creativity levels of the crafts displayed on stage was amazing. Then, it was over and she was walking to our table. Disappointment consumed me when she didn't immediately come to me. Maybe she was still angry that I hadn't called. I couldn't. Not in my state of confusion. Words may have been spoken that would later be regretted. Actions may have been taken that couldn't be undone. So before we had a conversation, I needed to be clear on what I wanted to do.

She didn't come to me. Instead...she went to Kyle. For the first time, I noticed how she fully exhaled when he encased her in his arms, how he rested his face in her hair and seemed to breathe in her scent. My heart raced. *Damn*...how did I not notice this before? Regardless of Kyle's fervent denials, it was apparent to me in this moment that he was in love with Toni. Absently, I ran my hands over my face. Every time I turn around, there's another monkey wrench in the plan. He and I had to have a conversation. Our relationship depended on it.

I felt eyes on me and turned to see Rae staring at me. She had witnessed it too. I saw the questions, and even surprise in her eyes. Hurriedly, I looked away. This situation was turning into one long nightmare.

Finally...release. She turned towards me then...me, her second choice. Still, I allowed her entrance into my arms, even with the lingering remnants of doubt. Looking over her head, I stared at Kyle, forcing him to look at me. The pretense was over. He didn't look away. Later. I turned to my lover.

"Toni, you guys did a wonderful job with the show tonight. I'm so proud of you."

"Yes Toni!" Rae chimed in. "The show was amazing. These kids are really talented. It's good to know that we are not losing all of our kids to the street."

"Thanks people. I'm proud of all of us, Tanya, Daniel, Mia…seems like all of our hard work is finally paying off."

She turned to me. "Thanks Keenan for coming. I really appreciate you being here." The raw honesty in her voice tugged at my heartstrings.

"You don't have to thank me, love. I'll always be here for you. How much longer do you have to be here? I'm kind of ready to have you to myself."

"Oh yeah?" she laughed. "Well I guess that's my cue to get this wrapped up. Let me check in with Tanya and Mia to see if they need anything else before I head out, then you can follow me home. Rae, can you follow me? Kyle, I will call you later."

"Sure. Keenan it was good seeing you." Rae stated. She looked at Kyle then back at me, sensing the tension between us. She turned to leave, following in Toni's footsteps.

Alone with my brother…there were no words between us. I broke the silence.

"You love her."

"Yes, Keenan I do. I just started to realize it, but I do."

I wanted to be angry but I couldn't. How could he let me love her knowing his feelings? Then again, I realized that I couldn't put the blame on him. In the beginning, he fought against the idea of "us", but we were determined to be together.

Me, fighting, even though I knew my circumstances. I alone was to blame.

"I love her too, Kyle."

He sighed. "I know that. But if you really love her, then choose her. If you don't, then I will."

"That's not fair."

"None of this is. But you created this, so it's up to you to fix it." With that he walked away, leaving me alone at the table. For the first time, I just simply felt alone.

....

Finally, home. Tired, but not completely exhausted. My body still wired from the excitement of the event. I wanted nothing more than to take a long bubble bath and have a cool glass of wine. Keenan had followed me home and I was glad about that. I knew we needed to talk, but I didn't want that yet. I didn't want to end the night with complications. I just wanted to relax, drink, and be loved.

I headed to the bath, while he went into the kitchen. As the steamy water filled the tub, I peeled my dress over my head and reached for a band to bind my hair. Just as my weary body was entering the warm, soothing water, Keenan appeared with my glass of wine. Graciously, I accepted it from him, before letting the water engulf me up to my neck. I took a long swallow of the liquid, relishing it's mildly sweet, cool taste on my tongue. The built-up tension from the past days gradually eased from my body. I closed my eyes.

"You want music?" I heard him ask. I nodded without opening my eyes. Soon the soulful, textured voice of India Arie echoed richly throughout the room. I heard him leave and felt his presence when he returned, which seemed to be no more than ten minutes later. Opening my eyes, I was surprised to find him almost completely undressed…almost, because he had chosen to keep on his boxers. Surprised, because his relationship status remained the elephant in the room that neither of us had, or was willing to address. When he followed me home from Muse, I really hadn't known what to expect. Would he be staying? Would we still be together?

I watched him with a fevered yearning… wanting so badly to invite him and all of his chocolate goodness into the water with me…to enjoy my moment, yet, I knew before we went "there" we needed to talk…to speak about our future…to determine if one even existed.

I finished the wine and carefully placed the glass on the floor. For a moment neither of us spoke.

"Would you like some more wine?" he asked quietly. The expression on his face was an indication that he was deep in thought. Not a good sign. I needed him to be at peace. To be completely sure that being with me was exactly where he wanted to be.

"No, not right now." I sank lower into the water, wishing to hide, knowing my efforts were futile. The steaming water, while useless as a protective shield, did serve its purpose of easing the tension from my back, neck, and shoulders. India Arie was now singing one of my favorite songs, "Heart of the Matter." Yes, India, we would definitely have to get down to the heart of it all before the night ended.

Finally, I emerged from the protective cloak of the water. Just as I stood, Keenan moved suddenly to grab my towel. Before wrapping it around my steamy, glistening body, he stared at me…so intently, so longingly, that my breath caught in my throat. How is it that this man could make me oh so weak at the knees?

Without much thought, I leaned towards him, having a sudden desire to taste his lips. Without hesitation, he discarded the towel and met me halfway, embracing me completely in his arms. I had missed him. Missed the feel of his naked body against my own skin. Missed his scent. At this moment, in the midst of inhaling him, loving him... I didn't care that another woman had his last name. Tonight he only belonged to me and that's all that matters.

His soft, full lips brushed against mine. Small kisses...gently tugging, gently pulling... gently biting. I pressed harder against him as a moan escaped my mouth. His manhood instantly hardened in response, evidence of his own growing arousal. He teased me with featherlike touches across the small of my back, the nape of my neck. He has learned these things about me, discovered the things that make me weak...makes me defenseless against his assault. I need to touch him. I grab his boxers and pull them down just enough for his engorged manhood to escape. He is so swollen that my hand appears deceptively small wrapped around him. There is an opposing tug of war that begins, him sucking, pulling my lips...me retaliating with firm grips and tugs. The intensity of our passion increases. Smothering in his kisses, I break away to come up for air. As I do so, his mouth finds other areas of interest...my jawline, the side of my neck. I become dizzy with my desire for him. I pull away completely and step out of the tub. Although I was still wet, I didn't bother to dry my body. I grabbed his hand and dragged him to my bed. Foreplay was over. I needed to feel him inside of me. As we got closer to the bed, he surprised me by grabbing me and flipping me on my stomach. Excitement coursed through every vein in my body. Without words, I knew what he wanted and exactly how he wanted it. Eagerly, I spread my legs...anticipating the feel of him. I felt his hands all over me...my hair, my back, my ass. I writhed and moaned...hungry and yearning.

"Please Keenan," I gasped.

"Please what? Tell me what you want."

"I…want… you", I moaned, feeling his sweet kisses on my back. My knees almost buckled when I felt the heat from his manhood press into my slick folds. I wanted to drown him in my juices, let him feel my need. His hands were in my hair, pulling me back towards him. Automatically, my body jerked in that sweet mixture of pain and pleasure. There was no gentleness in his movements. In the most primal way I could sense his hunger, smell it through his pores. His hands now on my thighs, spreading them wider. In one thrust he was inside. I screamed out, but there would be no mercy from my lover tonight. Every pent up frustration, every ounce of confusion and guilt…he gave to me in long hard strokes. There was a moment when I wanted to collapse, but he felt it and immediately increased his grasp on my hair. Tears poured down my face as I took in all of him, blow by blow. Tonight was a different kind of love. It was as if both of us knew that our lives would be forever changed after this moment. So we loved hard, body to body, sweat to sweat, moan to moan…until we cried out in a simultaneous climax.

I felt his soft breaths on my cheeks as he lay on top of me. His soft dreads caressed my face. Silently I wished that we could stay like this forever, but I knew better. This moment was only a temporary reprieve from the chaos that had become a constant fixture of our lives. At last, I felt his weight lift, and heard him walk into the bathroom. I heard the shower start. I got up and went to join him. Tomorrow, we would talk tomorrow.

....

My senses awakened to the tantalizing smells of breakfast and coffee. I got up and pulled on my jeans, which were recklessly strewn by the side of the bed. I twisted my dreads into a ponytail and headed into the kitchen.

Toni was just finishing up when I walked in. She was absolutely a beautiful sight in the mornings. As usual, her mass of curls were wild about her face, perfect, even without makeup. She had on a tiny pair of shorts that hugged her ass and an even smaller tee, which emphasized her small, ripe breasts.

"Hey love," she smiled when she noticed me. I walked up to her, wrapping her small frame up in my arms.

"Morning."

I released her and walked to the nook, laid out with the appealing spread. Very much in need of coffee, I poured a full cup from the carafe. She joined me and we began to eat.

We needed to talk, but not right now. I wanted to preserve this moment in my memory banks. Wanted to mentally capture and save the vision of her just as she is in this moment. I loved her so much. I never thought I could love a woman as much as I loved Sarai, but my heart was full with…no it was overflowing with my love for her. But…I would hurt her. Regardless of my intentions, without the issues between me and Sarai coming to a resolution, she was bound to get hurt. This was my dilemma.

We finished breakfast. While she cleared the table, I went to put on music. I heard her soft footsteps come into the room. From my peripheral, I watched her take up residence on the chaise…waiting.

I walked over and sat on the floor beneath her. Anxiety's presence marred her pretty face.

"So?" She asked softly. *Questions.*

"I love you." I needed her to know that. Wanted to reassure her.

"I'm going home." I stated simply in an effort to soften the blow. My efforts proved in vain, as her head snapped back as if I'd physically slapped her.

"Home?"

I'm not sure exactly when made the decision, but sometime between me and Sarai's last conversation, I resigned that I would give "us" another try. Maybe it was the consuming thoughts of my daughter or perhaps it was the sudden realization of Kyle's feelings. Somehow, I just realized that me and Toni were doomed if the existing, extenuating circumstances continued. I needed an escape. Sarai had invaded my sanctuary. The right thing to do was to go home, back to D.C…back to my daughter…and see if anything in our relationship could be salvaged. Admittedly, there was also a part of me that wanted to be sure that, once I was back in familiar territory, my feelings for Toni, would still be just as strong as they are right now. I also owed it to Kyle. If he really did love Toni, as much as I suspected he truly did, then I couldn't take her away from him based on false promises.

"Yes, Toni, I am so, so sorry, but I've decided that, just for a little while, I need to go back home, to get some resolution. I miss my daughter and need to see her. I owe it to her…to you…to Sarai to ensure that this marriage between us is really over. And as much as I love you, I know that being here, engulfed in "us" will not give me the opportunity to think as clearly as I need to."

Tears brimmed in her eyes before flowing down her face. *Pain.* Pain that I had once again caused. I just couldn't get this right.

"Oh my God," She laughed bitterly. "How could I be this dumb? Of course you're going home. I mean that's what you do right. You came here, running away from your troubles in D.C. and now that trouble has caught a plane and followed you, your only solution is to run away…yet again. Really, how crazy of me to expect that you would man up and handle your business. That you would stand up for me…for us." Her voice broke as she spit out the words. I knew that she would be upset, but I did not expect this much anger.

"You're nothing more than a coward in the truest form. And that's not the kind of man I need in my life…You know what Keenan, just get out! Get out!"

She stood up abruptly, brushing past me in her quest. She yanked her door open before any other words escaped my mouth.

"Toni, please let me explain."

"Explain? Are you serious? I cannot take…I won't take another lying, manipulative word coming out of your mouth. Leave my home."

Stunned by her response, I quickly gathered my shoes and the rest of my clothes that only a few short hours ago, had been scattered in our moment of ecstasy. She continued to stand by the door until I finished. Anger presented in her rigid stance. Still shocked, I felt my own emotions brewing and threatening to spill over. I knew that when I walked out that door, there was every bit the chance that she would not allow me back in. That knowledge hurt me in a very deep place.

There were no more words to be said. One day I hoped that she would forgive me. To understand why I made the choices I made…to realize the dilemma I faced. One day I hoped that she would understand the immense love I had…have for her. The imprint she made on my life. One day. Today, however, I was being forced to walk away from her, possibly be the greatest love of my life.

161

Chapter 18: Constant

It's amazing how even in the midst of unimaginable pain, the world never ceases to exist. Other lives seem to continue on their daily adventures, completely unaware of your own inner turmoil. I watched the same executives speeding by in their suits and sneakers, the same homeless people on the corners…the same students rushing to get food before their next classes.

One month. It had been exactly one month since I'd seen or heard from Keenan. One month since my world paused. One month of experiencing the same recurring nightmare. Somehow, I was still surprised that I ended up in this space. Even though I made the choice to date someone who was married, I really thought that Keenan would choose me. I believed that he loved me enough. How foolish of me to believe that our circumstances would be any different. I was "that" girl….again. Silly me.

Each day seemed to pass in a series of slow events. It was if I was navigating in a thick fog that I couldn't escape. I existed, yet, beyond that, there was nothing. There was an emptiness inside that nothing seemed to fill. This time I didn't hide. This time I reached out to my support system for the comfort I knew that they would give. In what could only be described as an ironic twist of fate, Dawn and Jamie had reconciled. Sort of. She and Lexie were still living with Rae, but they were trying to find their way back. At least twice a week they went out on dates, and he had begun spending more time with Lexie. I was excited for them…excited about their prospects. Still, I couldn't help feeling sorry for Craig, who had obviously fallen hard for Dawn. His chances were now put on indefinite hold. So much time, wastefully invested. Welcome to my world Craig, welcome to my world.

It was difficult for me to see Lexie reunited with Jamie. It seemed as if she and Dawn had both regained some of the light that had been dimmed in his absence. It was obvious that she had missed her daddy. How could Dawn not fight for that, for her little girl, even if not for herself? I understood now, why Sarai (she is real) felt it necessary to fly to Atlanta. She was making the choice to fight for her family, for her daughter's happiness. Thinking back on everything, I know I would have done the same. Doesn't mean that I no longer wanted him, Keenan, in my life. There's just a level of understanding that exists now that wasn't there before. The wars of women are many. Love, family, life, a never ending cycle.

The sudden ringing of my doorbell broke my meditative reverie. When I opened the door, I was pleasantly surprised. *Kyle.* I couldn't help smiling.

"Hey love." I spoke, walking into his open arms. Here was my foundation, my place of comfort. I wouldn't have made it through this ordeal without him. At this point, he was one of the few things in my life that I was sure of.

"Hey girl."

We moved from the doorway into the living room.

Before I sat down, I went into the kitchen to start another pot of coffee.

"What are you doing here Kyle? You know even though you're my best friend, you don't have to feel as if you're my babysitter too."

During this break-up period between me and Keenan, Kyle had really made an effort to be there for me. Not only was he checking on me and taking me out every weekend, he also stopped by the store during his free time. It had been a long time since we had spent this much quality time together. Sometimes, even against my wishes, he would stay long enough to assist me with closing. His presence eased my pain...somewhat. At the very least, being around him kept me from being lonely.

Unfortunately, spending so much time with me had cost him his developing relationship with Stacy. He should've listened to me. I warned him that no woman wanted to play seconds to another woman, regardless of the relationship. A shame too, because we had finally met and I discovered that I actually liked her as a potential mate for him. She proved not to be like the typical women Kyle usually had hanging on his arm. She was very beautiful, smart, and ambitious. Recently, she had opened a salon and had managed to score some high class clientele. I found her as someone who could complement and enhance Kyle's life...not someone to try and use him for a certain lifestyle.

She seemed to genuinely care for him, and it seemed as if he felt the same, but there were arguments and misunderstandings, which seemed to always revolve around me. I begged him to let go before he lost the best relationship I've known him to have. But he never walked away. Instead, beyond frustrated, Stacy was the one who walked. Even unintentional, I always seemed to complicate this man's life. Yet, here he was, now curled up on my sofa, waiting for coffee...loving me still. What more could a girl ask for?

"I know, I know. You're probably sick to death of my face by now, but since you ran off my girlfriend you owe me." He teased.

"Kyle...don't say that," I pouted. "You know I feel responsible for what happened between you and Stacy."

"You know I love teasing you. Why do you keep blaming yourself for that? Not your fault. We just didn't work. You were only a small part of the equation. Believe me."

I fixed two cups of coffee, giving him one of them when I walked back into the room.

"Yeah well, I can't help but to blame myself. I seem to have a bad habit of interfering and destroying other people's relationships. If karma really is the bitch that everyone claims she is, then I fear her vengeance on me."

"Oh God, please stop being so dramatic. Anyway, that's even more proof that you need me by your side. Who else is going to be patient enough to deal with you bumbling through life?"

We both laughed, which felt really good to my soul. The heavy clouds that shadowed my earlier mood slowly began to dissipate.

We talked, catching up with the week's events. He talked about his upcoming cases. I talked about Muse's upcoming events. We talked until our eventual hunger threatened to overtake us. Deciding to go to lunch, we drove to Millie's, his favorite BBQ place. Although I didn't need the extra calories, I did look forward to drowning my face in spicy bbq sauce, ribs, sweet tea, and sweet potato pie. Nothing like the comfort of southern food to ease a broken heart.

Even though it was the weekend, it wasn't very busy. I grabbed a table as Kyle ordered our food. Minutes later, he was at the table brandishing our number. Small talk again until our food arrived. Then, absolute silence, while we devoured every morsel on our plates. In this moment I was glad that I was with him. There were no pretenses as I ate and licked my lips and my fingers. At one point, he watched me, laughed, then reached over and wiped my mouth with his napkin.

"So uncivilized."

I laughed. "Shut up. You love my uncivilized ass."

Suddenly he became somber. "Yeah…yeah I do." There was a different look in his eyes as he watched me. I couldn't explain it. It was just different. Suddenly, in the recesses of my mind, a memory was retrieved. A memory of Dawn telling me that Kyle had feelings for me. That thought seemed crazy…foolish at the time, yet, the look in his eyes at this moment was definitely different.

I spoke, if only to ease the mounting tension.

"You know I really like this place. I swear they have the best ribs, at least on this side of town."

He leaned back in his chair and looked around aimlessly. "Yeah…love it on nights when they have a live band. You know the last time I was here was with Keenan, when he told me about your 'relationship'."

Keenan. I didn't expect to hear his name today. Not from Kyle. Usually he avoided mentioning his name, knowing the hurt that I was still experiencing.

"Well friend, I certainly wish you had done a better job of talking him out of it."

"Ah it didn't matter. I begged him to leave it alone, leave you alone…but I knew from talking to him that it was too late. He had gotten to know you, and to know you is…well is to love you." He purposely made eye contact when he spoke those last words and I caught my breath. There was a sudden realization that today our relationship would change…leaving me in a state of panic. I wasn't prepared for this. Kyle was my constant. I wouldn't be able to handle it if our relationship was altered.

I broke our contact, looking down into my empty dish.

"How is he?" I asked quietly. Not even sure if I truly wanted to know the answer.

"You really want to know?"

I looked up into his questioning face. "Yeah, I at least want him to be ok. I love him…so there is a part of me that will always hope that he's happy, even if he's not with me."

For a moment, he was silent. "Honestly, he's struggling Toni. They are trying but it's been difficult." I was actually surprised to hear this. When he made the choice to leave, I believed it was him choosing not only Zy'riah, but Sarai. That somehow he realized that there was a part of him that was still loving her.

"Do you think I'm the cause?"

"Yes. Of course part of the problem is the fact that their issues were never resolved, but I know him. He will never be able to love Sarai the same as before because he still loves you. There is a part of him that still wants to be with you."

Before that information could be fully digested, a waiter came to clear our table. As soon as she left, he turned back to me with a serious expression on his face.

"Toni, do you still love him?"

Why would he ask me that? Didn't he already know the answer? It was too soon. One month was not nearly enough time to erase the love I had for Keenan.

"Yes Kyle, of course I do. I probably always will. None of that matters though because he didn't choose me."

Silence. I no longer wanted to have this conversation. I wanted to go back to a couple of hours ago, when we were being silly…laughing. This was too serious for me to handle. I just needed for him to be my constant.

"Are you ready?" He asked without any further mention of Keenan. I nodded slightly and we immediately left the restaurant.

The rest of the day passed smoothly. We grabbed coffee from a local shop then walked around Centennial Park. It was a beautiful September day, despite a chill that had been left in the aftermath of a weeklong rainstorm. Due to the sudden drop in temperature, there were no kids playing in the infamous Olympic fountains, however; their presence was visible in the playground area. Seeing them, dressed in a mirage of colorful scarves and jackets, I realized that the summer was officially over. Somehow, without my detection, it had passed while I was all wrapped up in the relationship with Keenan.

We located a bench and drank our coffee as we people-watched. There were countless families encroached upon the park. In one area, a soccer game was in development, in another, what appeared to be a father and son, were carelessly tossing a football about. Nearby, a young couple, obviously in the throes of a first love were making out…kissing, whispering, touching. Reminiscent of loves past. Back when love was innocent and not complicated by the factions of life. I couldn't help wondering if one day I would be here…perhaps with a family of my own…maybe casually enclosed in the arms of my lover. One day maybe.

There was a serious conversation to be had between Kyle and myself about our relationship, but not now. Not in this moment. Right now I just wanted to lose myself in the display of life spread before me. Leaning over, I found a comfortable spot to rest my head on his shoulder. As he has done a thousand times before, he wrapped his arm around me. *Constant.*

Chapter 19: Home Again

One month. One month since I'd last spoken to Toni. One month since I'd heard that sultry voice...seen her beautiful face...walked out. One month of regret. To say that this reconciliation was not working would be an understatement. No matter how hard I tried, I could not fully commit to Sarai. The past few months have left me emotionally bankrupt. I have nothing left to give. To her at least. The mistake I made was in thinking that my heart could be done with Toni. Clearly it was not. I thought those two weeks of separation had been tough; it was nothing in comparison to the misery that I have experienced in the last thirty days. My body ached for her...yearned for her. My spirit felt her absence. If I had known it would be like this, I would have never walked out of her door. But I had. Now, I was here, back to my beginnings. Miserable in my present.

Through it all though, I have to admit that being reunited with Zy'riah has been rewarding. I hadn't realized how much I had missed our routine life. Her incessant laughter and talking. Her joy and excitement at the simplest things in life that only a child could have. I knew she missed me. Since I've been home, she rarely leaves my side. Like today. Today I was on the way for a much needed visit to see my parents. As soon as she saw me pick up my keys, she ran to get her jacket. I could've used the time alone on the drive, but there was no denying my baby.

As we walked to the van, I was struck by the irony at how my life as a family man had returned. From Sonoma pickup to mini-van. Just like that. I called my dad when I got on the road to let him know that we were on the way. He was excited to know that Zy'riah was with me...I don't think they had seen much of her in my absence. I heard him relay the message to my mom and her excitement was also evident.

Ten minutes later we were in my old neighborhood. Sometimes I still can't believe that I chose to live so close. There were two main reasons that factored into our decision. First, as an only child, I wanted to be close to my parents as they started aging. Being near them allowed me to not only take care of my own home, but to help dad with chores around theirs as well. It was a lot of responsibility but I was happy to help. Especially during the time when I had quit my job. It gave me the opportunity to keep busy and to steer clear of Sarai when things started to go south. I also wanted to be near them because it was important to me for them to have a great relationship with their only grandchild. They loved her to pieces and spoiled her rotten. The funny thing is, she spent more time with my dad that she did with my mom. Many times he would stop by the house on his way to run errands to pick her up to go with him. She once told me that granddad was her best friend like Uncle Kyle was mine. Gotta love kids.

From a glance, everything in the neighborhood appeared just as it was throughout my childhood and adulthood. Most of the homes were modest and traditional. Many of the families have been here for years, although recently there had been a few deaths of some of the older members like Ms. Ruth. Ms. Ruth was the legendary neighborhood candy lady. As young boys Kyle and I would spend just about every dime we earned from chores, allowances, odd jobs...all on Ms. Ruth's treats. We would stock up then head back to my stoop to eat our stash. We only shared with other kids if there were cute girls that we were trying to impress. I laughed, thinking about those simple times. I missed those days. And Ms. Ruth. She passed away two years ago. All of my life she had sat on that front stoop nosily watching the kids, yelling at us if she caught us in mischief, alerting us if she had something special, like ice-cream for that day. As I thought about her, I slowly drove past her house, blue with freshly painted white trim.

Good to see that her son, Ricky, was still keeping the house in good condition. He and his wife had moved in with Ms. Ruth when her health began to decline. Ricky, like me, was an only child who shouldered all of the responsibility for his parent's care. I never knew Ms. Ruth's husband, who I was told, died a few years before my birth. I always questioned why she never remarried in all of those years. Boyfriends yes, at least when I was younger, but she never allowed another man to live in her husband's home. Mom said that even though Mr. Ricky Sr. had passed, Ms. Ruth always had a sense of loyalty to him. As if it would be a betrayal if she took another man's name. Crazy, but in some ways, something to be respected.

My house, well my parent's home, was at the end of the street. It was small yellow house with black shutters, modest, but certainly enough for the three of us. True to form, my dad was outside standing, waiting for us to arrive. It's amazing how tall he is considering the fact that I'm averaged height at best. He had on his customary khakis and a long-sleeved shirt. My dad was an honest, proud man, something you could see just by watching him. Traditional in his values, even though his family had moved from the south many moons ago.

Zy'riah was barely out of her booster before she ran, jumping into his arms. He laughed at her child-like enthusiasm. I gathered our belongings, walked up the steps, and gave my dad a hug.

"Hey Pops."

"Hey son." Still carrying Zy'riah, he turned and walked into the house where my mom was waiting. I followed close behind. The house smelled deliciously sweet. Obviously my mom had started baking cookies when she knew we were coming. Of course I knew it wasn't for my benefit. I stopped being the baby the moment my daughter was born.

She came bounding out of the small kitchen, a wide grin plastered on her beautiful face. I smiled back. My mother is small in stature, but carries a great presence. She kissed me on the cheek and reached for Zy'riah.

"Hello son."

"Hey Mom." I'd missed my parents. This was another good thing about being back at home. Getting to spend quality time with them on a regular basis.

Before we could talk more, Zy'riah interrupted, "Grandma you making cookies?"

My mom laughed, "Yes baby, I'm making your favorite…sugar cookies…come on with me in the kitchen so we can finish them." I'll even let you put the icing on them." Zy'riah hurriedly got out of her jacket and gave it to me before bouncing into the kitchen. I shook my head, giving my mom a stern look.

"You know you spoil her right?"

"Oh hush…that's my only grandbaby…of course I'm going to spoil her." With that she turned and purposefully walked back into the kitchen. I turned to my dad who just smiled and shrugged his shoulders. Why was I even trying to fight this battle?

I made myself comfortable on the worn patterned sofa, while my dad took his usual spot in his adjacent recliner. There wasn't room for much conversation as the afternoon games were on, including a game between his beloved Redskins and their division rivals the Dallas Cowboys.

By the time the game was over, the cookies had all been baked and cooled and Zy'riah had eaten her fair share. She was noticeably wired after her indulgence, so my mom decided to walk her down the street to the neighborhood park so she could exert some of her energy. I would've walked with them but I could tell that my mom wanted some alone time with her grandchild. I let them go on their way.

They weren't gone long before Pops turned to me with a certain look on his face, which I knew meant that he wanted to talk. What about I didn't know.

"So son, everything going alright?" he asked. Ok, so that's what this conversation would be about. I sighed. I wasn't really in the mood to have a discussion about me and Sarai, but I knew that his stubbornness would not allow him to just drop the subject. My dad was an old school family man. He and my mom have had their ups and downs, but he believed that a man's responsibility was to preserve the family unit. He was disappointed and angry in my decision to move to Atlanta. In his view, I was abandoning my family…unable to comprehend how desperately I needed the escape. For the months that I was in Atlanta, we barely spoke. My pleas and explanations did little to soften his impenetrable resolve. His love for me never diminished, but it was obvious that, in my absence, he didn't like me very much. I was not acting like the man he raised me to be.

Since moving back our relationship has steadily improved. But I'm sure he could sense that matters were still not resolved in my household. I was trying, but I was not happy. Happy to be reunited with my daughter…but the sense of "happiness" was something that was still elusive in my marriage. I was getting back to that place where my soul was not at peace. And I'm just not sure I can live the rest of my life this way. Not for my daughter, for my father, or Sarai.

"The truth Pops…it's all still a work in progress."

Without his glance wavering he continued to pry, "But there is progress?"

I wasn't going to lie to him. "Honestly Pops, very little. I'm trying the best I can to love Sarai like she deserves to be loved, but I'm just not there anymore. I don't know if I can get back there. It's like we lost our common ground."

He looked away briefly and I could tell that he was in deep thought. I knew that this conversation would only lead to his further disappointment, but it had to be said, he had to know.

"Is it that woman in Atlanta?"

Toni. Admittedly, Toni was still an obstacle. I wanted to see if I could bury our relationship in the recesses of my mind. Wanted to see if I could not love her, not think of her. But every attempt had been a failure. Our moments together were so special…they proved difficult to recapture or emulate, even with the woman I had spent the last decade loving. Her voice, her skin, her words, her love…have woven themselves into my being. It was proving impossible to let her go. If I couldn't let her go, how was I going to have a meaningful life with Sarai? It would be a fraud.

"Somewhat." I whispered, not wanting to deal with his reaction. I witnessed the sudden slump in his shoulders. Heard his breath escape in a long sigh. Suddenly, he shifted and pushed his way out of the recliner. He didn't say a word as he left and ambled down the long hallway, seemingly towards their bedroom. He was gone for about thirty minutes before he returned with a piece of paper that had been withered and aged by time and creases. He held it out to me and I took it with reservation.

As I unfolded it, I realized that it was a copy of him and mom's marriage license. I couldn't help but to smile. So he was going to pull out the big guns huh. I had never seen the document. It was a little strange seeing the evidence of their union. Forty years seemed like forever. How had they made it last when me and Sarai were struggling to get to a decade.

"Why are you showing me this Pop? What does this mean?"

He had settled back comfortably in his recliner.

"Son, the day I married your mom, I meant my vows as forever. It hasn't been all roses, it hasn't been without trouble, anger, disappointment…hurt. But I've never doubted my choice of her as my wife. I've never dishonored my vows. That piece of paper is not just worthless ink, despite what you young folks think. That paper symbolizes my promise to the state, to your mother, to God. You can't just cut the cords when the rough patches hit. You stay, you fight. That's the commitment that paper requires. That's what a man does."

His impassioned plea brought unexpected tears to my eyes. The last thing I wanted was to be less of a man than my father expected…demanded. But he never doubted his choice, when I had every bit of doubt in mine. Even now, anyone who witnessed my mother and father together knew that they were still madly in love with each other. There were glances, gestures, touches…words unspoken and declared. I couldn't see me and Sarai sitting in the rocking chairs on the stoop. That vision had long since dimmed. That kind of love between us had long since waned. Wouldn't a man also know when to walk away?

Wordlessly, I gave my dad back the certificate. I stood and walked out of the door, down the steps, and continued down the street. I was going to get my daughter from the park. Then, I was going home.

Chapter 20: Confessions Part Two

Home. Finally. After a very long Saturday at the store. Exhausted. Midterms at the local colleges kept us busy with students cramming for their exams. Individuals, study groups…we had them all, including our regular customers. I wasn't complaining. The busier I am, the less time I have for thinking, or overthinking.

No sooner had I walked through the door when my cell rang. *Dawn.*

"Hey girl," I answered as I crash landed on the nearest sofa. She was calling to see if I wanted to go out for dinner and bowling with the crew. Although I was in desperate need of entertainment, I was just too exhausted to do anything more than take a hot shower and have a marathon movie night. Understanding, she let me go without a fight, promising to call me later when they reached the bowling center, just in case I changed my mind.

Ah what a difference a few months can make. It seemed like such a long time ago that I was club hopping and serial dating on the scene, now here I was, homebound on a Saturday. Not lonely, yet still alone. I headed to the kitchen to pour my first glass of wine, and then headed to the bathroom to start my shower. I undressed and stepped into the welcoming heat. After a few minutes of allowing the pulsing hot water to massage my weary body, I got out, wrapping myself in a freshly warmed robe. I grabbed my now empty glass and padded back into the kitchen for a refill. This felt like a Love Jones kind of evening.

Locating the DVD, I popped it in and settled on the chaise for the start of my night of relaxation. Just when the situation between Darius and Nina were about to heat up, the doorbell rang. *Damn.* I definitely wasn't expecting anyone so it took me by surprise. After a brief glance through keyhole, I opened the door and headed back to the chaise. Kyle strolled in behind me, closing the door as he entered.

Usually, seeing his face would have made my night, but ever since our last outing, things between us have been uncomfortable, to say the least. I wasn't kidding myself any longer. The emotions that I was seeing from him were real. I couldn't say exactly what those feelings were, but I now knew that Dawn's earlier projections were on point. Kyle no longer saw me as just his best friend. And I hadn't quite figured out what to do with this realization. We should have discussed it by now; yet again the coward side of me was winning the battle. This...I can't handle this right now. Kyle is my constant, and emotionally I can't afford to have this piece of my life altered in any way. Selfish...yes. I didn't care anymore. Life was teaching me that self-preservation was more important. And that's exactly what I needed to do...save myself.

Wordlessly, I curled back on the chaise and watched him. What was he doing here anyway? Based on my conversation with Dawn I knew that he was a part of the bowling/dinner crew. But here he was standing in my living room...watching me, watching him.

"What are you doing here Kyle? If you came to rescue me, don't. You don't always have to be my hero."

The impact of my words stung. I could tell by the wince on his face. I had never spoken to him in that manner before and I'm sure he was stunned at hearing them now.

"Wow, that's probably the worst welcome I've ever received coming here. You want to tell me what the problem is?

And yes I did come by to rescue you. When Dawn told me that you weren't coming out tonight, I decided to come over so that you wouldn't be spending yet another night alone. As your friend, I'm not going to allow you to become this isolated hermit. Keenan is gone. You need to remember that you had a life here before him."

As he spoke the pitch of his voice rose, indicative of his anger. Thinking back, I couldn't remember the last time Kyle was angry with me. I felt the sting of tears in my eyes, at the sudden realization of just how much my life had fallen apart in only a matter of months. The man I loved had left me. My relationship with my best friend was in shambles. I was disconnected from my family and friends. I was at the lowest point in my life. And I was powerless to do anything about it.

"You don't want me here?" He asked dejectedly. He moved to sit next to me on the chaise, but unlike other times, he didn't make a move to touch me in any way. No kisses, no hugs. I turned to look at his handsome profile. I could see the strain etched across his face; saw the clenching of his jawline. I never wanted to hurt him in any way.

"Kyle…do you love me?" Stillness. I thought he wasn't going to answer me. I wasn't even certain that I deserved an answer.

"Yes Toni," he sighed, turning to look at me face to face. "I have loved you…been in love with you since the first day I met you. Since the first day I saw you on campus with your big afro of curls. Since the first time I heard you laugh, the first time you cried on my shoulder, since the first time you recited your beautiful words of poetry to me. I have loved you through it all, and I am still in love with you."

Tears bathed my face as I allowed his words to digest. There it was, in the atmosphere. Kyle loved me. Not as his best friend, but as a man truly loves a woman. He was now free from that burden, but now that weight had been transferred to me. I felt their heaviness…maybe too heavy for me to carry. I didn't, couldn't lose my best friend. But I couldn't love him back, not like he needed to be loved. Keenan still had a grip on my heart. Even with him not choosing me, even with him living another life, with another woman…my heart still was holding on to him…and it wouldn't be fair to Kyle to give him false hope.

"Why didn't you tell me? All of these years…all of the men who broke my heart…you let me love them…you let me love Keenan…if you had this to offer, why didn't you offer it to me all of those times when I needed it the most, when there was the possibility that I could love you back?"

"Because I wasn't ready, Toni. I loved you, but I was not ready to give you the commitment you deserved. I could have been selfish, I could have had you on hold waiting for me, but I've always loved you too much to do that. I just assumed that when I was ready you would be there. I knew that what I did have to offer, no one else could give you, but I never planned on Keenan." He laughed slightly, "That was the greatest monkey wrench life could have thrown me. When I saw you together I knew that I would lose you. And I didn't plan for that. Trust me, this will probably be the biggest regret I'll have."

I leaned on his shoulder…even now in the midst of this new crisis, I needed him. Needed to be comforted by all that was familiar, his scent…the feel of his arms. Sensing my mood, he wrapped me up and began stroking my loose curls. I closed my eyes, welcoming his forbidden touch. I felt light kisses on my forehead…down my jaw. I sensed his slight hesitation before I felt his soft lips press against my own. I should have been pushing him away, off of this destructive path… instead, I let him in…I needed him.

When I didn't back away, he kissed me again, this time pulling my bottom lip into the warmth of his mouth. Small nibbles sent tiny quakes throughout my body. This was different. I hadn't kissed another man besides Keenan in almost a year. The passion wasn't the same, but it was exhilarating none the less. He was still being cautious…waiting for me to retreat. Instead, I offered him the taste of my tongue. He groaned as his hunger elevated to another level. I grabbed the sides of his face, pulling him in closer. He answered by pulling my hair back, allowing him greater access to my mouth, my neck, the base of my throat. His mouth was everywhere. My own moans escaped my lips as he ravished me. This was a man who loved me, who wanted me. How could I deny him? How could I deny myself?

He finally pulled back, leaving us both gasping for air. He closed his eyes, but still reached up to touch my face. I took the opportunity to kiss his long fingers, kiss the palm of his hand.

"Toni," he asked, eyes still closed…"are you sure? Is this what you want? Am I who you want?"

Silence. I couldn't answer him…I didn't know how to answer him. I still wanted Keenan… this I was sure of. But I was also sure that I needed him. I needed to feel connected, loved, wanted. Everything about this was wrong, but for tonight I wanted to be selfish. I wanted to receive what he never was able to offer before. Tonight that would be enough.

He opened his eyes to look at me. There was such longing that it broke my heart. Tears again. He sighed while he tenderly wiped them away. He leaned over and kissed me softly on my forehead.

"I got you baby."

He reached around to the base of my neck…his right hand holding me firmly in place while he deftly untied my robe with his left. My body tingled with excitement and anticipation. When I got out of the shower, I had only put on my underwear with the robe, so there were no other barriers once the robe was discarded. My erect nipples greeted him. He stared for a minute. I have never seen him in this light before, never seen him as a sexual, pleasurable being. Tonight, he was not my best friend, he was all man…and I wanted him. He laid me back on the chaise, before unbuttoning his shirt and pulling his t-shirt over his head. *Different.* Lean and muscular, unlike Keenan's sculpted thickness. Caramel instead of chocolate. Both obscenely beautiful. He didn't remove his jeans as I expected him to. Instead, he leaned over and kissed my bare stomach. Light kisses around my navel, then a trail up to that hollow place between my breasts. I closed my eyes and tried to lose myself in the moment, tried to forget all of the events and drama of the past months…tried to forget the repercussions that would exist when this night was over.

His mouth and hands traveled to my breasts. While kneading them gently, he began to sample each nipple. His touch was achingly sweet as he sucked each one, bringing them back to erection. I whimpered as I grabbed the back of his head. He lifted his head and kissed me again, gently rubbing his thumb over my nipples. Still kissing me, his hands moved lower, as if my heat was drawing him in. He tugged at my underwear and I lifted my body so that he could pull them down over my legs. Again, he stopped long enough to stare at me. His longing gaze caressed every inch of my brown skin. Then he reached out, into my heated, wet folds and finished the journey his eyes began. I cried out as he gently massaged me. With every stroke of his finger, his lips simultaneously tugged at my nipple, creating ripples of exquisite sensations. I squirmed beneath his assault. I grabbed his hand attempting to pull him in deeper, wanting to ease the ache that had settled in the pit of my belly. I felt myself getting closer to climax. Felt the wave beginning to overpower me. I tried pulling his body closer, tugging at his jeans so that his manhood could escape and rescue me. But he just kept massaging, kept stroking…seemingly focused on the task at hand. Furiously he worked until my clit was swollen and ready to erupt. A sheen of sweat now coated my body. I cried out begging for him to give me more. But he held firm until finally, my orgasm hit me wave after wave...leaving me in a sated pool of ecstasy.

There were light kisses on my thighs and belly before he pulled up next to me on the chaise. He wrapped my robe around my still trembling body and drew me into his arms. As the high of my climax dissipated, the state of my new reality hit me. Where could we go from here? Could our friendship be salvaged? How could we move forward with any relationship with the shadow of Keenan's ghost lingering?

He spoke, "You good?"

How was I to answer that? My body felt amazing, but my spirit was fragmented. I didn't know who this woman was anymore. A woman who would sleep with a married man. A woman who would sleep with her best friend, who coincidentally was her lover's best friend. I didn't even know how to begin to get back to "good". Any good intentions I started with disappeared a long time ago.

Still I answered "yes".

"Good, get some sleep." He grabbed my throw from the back of the sofa and covered me.

"What about you? Are you good?" I gazed at him with questions in my eyes, trying to get a read on his emotions. But his earlier transparency was lost. In its place was the stark expression he typically wore when he was Kyle, the attorney, and not Kyle my best friend.

He laughed slightly. "I will be Toni. Don't worry about me. I just wanted to give you what you needed. When I take complete possession of you it will be when you belong to me and I know that you love me back. Until then, I will be as good as I can be."

I stared at this man. Kyle, my constant…always unselfish, always loving me in spite of myself. The irony of life seemed especially cruel. I should have been loving him first. Instead, my heart was still held captive to a man that was loving someone else.

Chapter 21: All In…

I woke up the next morning around 10 a.m., a late-start for me. Kyle was already gone, which was somewhat of a relief. I don't think that I was prepared to face him after last night's events. After another shower, I made a pot of coffee and called Rae. I needed to vent about what had happened, about Kyle's profession of love. Too many thoughts were clouding my head and I needed to talk them out in order to make any sense of it all. After the fourth ring, she finally answered. After hearing the grogginess in her voice, I remembered that they had been out the night before, drinking, eating, having fun…all while my life was coming apart at the seams. Maybe I should have gone out with them. Perhaps I could have avoided this new "situation".

"Rae wake up I need to talk to you." I pleaded.

"Toni, it's too freakin early in the morning. This better be an emergency."

Maybe not for her…certainly so by my definition. I needed to find order out of this chaos.

"Do you really think I would be calling you at this hour if it wasn't? Look, I really need to talk to you. Can we do lunch. I need some food and some wine"

"That serious huh," she laughed. "Ok let's do a mutual spot. How about Cat's at Atlantic Station.? That way I can shop when we're finished. I'm long overdue for a new pair of boots."

After agreeing to meet at noon, we hung up...her to finish sleeping, me to finish thinking. My thoughts were running rampant. It's unbelievable that I would find myself here...in the midst of another crisis. Just months ago my life seemed so much simpler. Now, I didn't even feel like the same person I used to be.

I read and listened to music for another hour before dressing and hurrying out of the door. I didn't want to hear Rae's mouth about me being late. Not today. With traffic and the almost impossible task of finding parking, I walked into Cat's at a quarter after our designated time. All of my efforts proved to be in vain.

Cat's is a small café so when I walked in I had no trouble spotting Rae, who was already seated at a small table near the bar. I could tell by the look on her face that she was annoyed by my usual tardiness. Even so, she stood to greet me with a hug. I greeted her with my usual litany of apologies.

"Damn Toni," she scolded, "how is it that you cannot ever seem to be on time. I knew I should have left the house later than I did." Silently I let her vent and rant. Arguing would prove to be futile anyway. Our waiter appeared just as she was winding down. We both ordered salads and I ordered a bottle of Chardonnay for the both of us. One glass wouldn't be sufficient for the conversation that was about to take place.

"So," she began. "What was so important that you had to disturb my beauty sleep?"

I paused before answering her. Just a few short hours ago I was ready to spill my heart out, but there was another part of me that wasn't ready to tackle any of the blame and judgment that was to come. Besides where should the story begin? Did it really begin last night at my house or had it already been in progress? On the drive over I thought long and hard about Kyle's confession. I had to admit that deep down I knew Kyle's feelings for me. I knew it each moment he held me, each time he wiped my tears…saw it on his face the night I left the club with Keenan. It was there in so many subtle ways. Like Dawn said, maybe it was just easier to live in a state of denial. At some point those feelings were bound to surface. The timing though, couldn't be worse.

I began with Kyle's profession of love, which did not seem to surprise her. What did surprise her was my confession about me and Kyle's sexual act. I almost held on to that information, but it had been eating away at me ever since it happened, and I no longer wanted to carry the weight of that burden alone.

Her face registered shock as well as disappointment as the words poured from my mouth. "Toni, you didn't?"

Yes. Yes I did. There was a brief interruption as the waiter brought the wine and served it up in two glasses. Before continuing I took a long sip, noticing that Rae did as well.

"How could you do that to him Toni, how could you let that happen?" Her voice was an angry whisper, something I was not expecting. Do to HIM? Did she not understand that Kyle invited himself to my house and put this burden on me? What exactly did I do to him?

"Wait a minute…why are you angry at me? I didn't ask for all of this. I keep getting these bombs dropped on my doorstep and I'm left to figure out how to detonate them. This is not on me Rae."

Another long sip and I was ready for glass number two. Our salads came and we allowed a few moments of silence as we began eating. I had never doubted that Rae would be disappointed but her anger surprised me. It stung. With Keenan no longer a part of my life and my relationship with Kyle in turmoil, the last thing I need is for things to get sour between us.

After a few bites, I leaned back in my seat and settled my gaze on her…waiting for her response. I didn't have long to wait.

"Look Toni, I'm not blaming you for this situation with Keenan. But I am blaming you for allowing things to even get that far with Kyle. Granted, he probably could've chosen a better time, but I'm sure he's been hurting having to watch your relationship develop with Keenan. What I need for you to remember though is that he's not just some guy off of the streets that can be used as a seat-filler. He's Kyle…our friend…your best friend. There is no good that can come from allowing him to get mixed up in this situation, especially when it's so evident that you are still in love with Keenan."

Of course that's the last thing I wanted. But I couldn't fix this now. The damage had been done. I felt the sting of tears in my eyes. Sensing the shift in my mood, my friend reached across the table and held my hand. I could see the curious looks on the faces of the nearby patrons.

"Come on, girl. You know I'm hard but I'm honest. And my honest advice is: If you can't love him back fully, completely…don't cross that line. You may find yourself at a point of no return. And even though he works my nerves sometimes, there's no denying that he's much too valuable for you to lose."

"I know that you're right, Rae. I never thought that meeting Keenan, being with him could have this kind of impact on my life. I just feel that I've lost so much in these past few months. I'm so confused right now. It wouldn't be fair to try and have a relationship with Kyle, knowing my feelings for Keenan still exist, but at some point I have to move on. At some point, I have to come to terms with the fact that he's not coming back. So why should I not give an opportunity to a man that could truly love me. Who wants to be with me?"

"But Kyle deserves all of you, Toni. You know that. He doesn't deserve to be loved less than absolutely. If you can't give him that…leave your friendship intact."

As always she was giving me truth that I couldn't deny. Either I was going to be in or out with Kyle, there was no room for gray areas. I had to take the time to make the best decision possible because Rae was correct in that I could not afford to lose him. Even the thought of not having him in my life was enough to send me into a near anxiety attack.

After we finished our meals, I paid for the both of us hoping to appease her annoyance at me being late. Shopping was next on our agenda. The mood lightened considerably as we laughed and gossiped while trying on clothes and shopping for jewelry and boots. The excursion took much longer than expected so after a couple of hours we took a break to have dessert and coffee. I was thankful that we had this time alone. I needed my friend and as always, getting her point of view left me with a greater sense of clarity. It was time to get my act together. In or Out?

Chapter 22: …Or Out?

So far today was a good day. Finally. After the conversation with my Pops, I decided to really put forth an effort to make this work with Sarai. Remarkably, she had actually been responding to my efforts. Last night I recruited my parents to babysit while I prepared a romantic night. When she arrived home from a late night at the office, I had prepared dinner complete with fresh flowers and scented candles. Surprise, as well as elation registered on her face. I couldn't blame her. I hadn't been the easiest person to deal with lately. Living with my heart split in two places was proving to be a challenge. It was hard to focus on my marriage when my thoughts were somewhere else…with someone else. But I promised her that I would try…and she at least deserved a whole hearted effort in that.

After dinner we had wine, listened to music and watched movies. For the first time in a long time it felt good spending time with her. There were even moments when it felt like the first time we started dating. Exciting, fresh, fun. We made love…not sex but really made love. There were slow kisses, massages, touches. Admittedly, there was a brief, crazy moment when I felt guilty, thinking somehow that I was betraying Toni. Fortunately, I was able to push that thought aside and enjoy being with my wife. Truthfully, the passion wasn't comparable to what Toni and I shared, but it was good again. Really good. Which is why today has been a good day.

We went to collect Zy'riah from my parents, but they insisted that she spend the day with them. From the look in my father's eye, I surmised that this was just a ploy to allow me and Sarai to have more time together. I couldn't even be mad. It was just good to be back in his good graces.

There was no specific plan established. We found a local spot to eat brunch, then decided to hit some stores to do a little shopping. Time was passing by so quickly. Thanksgiving was just around the corner and Christmas would soon be breathing down our necks. My phone rang just as we were about to take a dessert and coffee break. *Kyle*. I gave Sarai my order then walked outside before answering.

"Keenan," I answered. It had been a couple of weeks since Kyle and I had last spoken. Our relationship, as was the rest of my life, was a work in progress. My discovery of his love for Toni had changed our dynamics, but he was my cousin, my "brother" and those ties forged a strong bond.

"What's good cousin?" was his reply. There was small talk about family and work before getting to the exact nature of his call.

"Keenan, I went by to get your mail from the landlord. He reminded me that your lease would be up in a couple of months. Are you gonna renew it?"

Not knowing how long I would be in Atlanta, I signed a six-month lease on my apartment instead of the usual year lease. When I moved back to D.C. I paid my rent two months ahead. I could have paid out the lease and terminated the contract, but I honestly didn't know how things were going to transpire with Sarai, so I opted to keep it. It was a source of argument for me and Sarai. In her mind, the fact that I was choosing to keep the apartment was a sign that I wasn't truly committed to making our marriage work. In the beginning, she was probably right. I needed to keep my options open. The apartment in Atlanta was my gateway to Toni and I wasn't ready to close that door yet. Now, though, the time had come for me to make a final decision. Now that I was home was I staying? Was I finally ready to release my hold on Toni?

"Thanks man. Let me think about it and I'll give you a final decision by the end of the week."

There was a moment of silence. I asked the question I had been dreading to ask. "How is she Kyle?"

I heard his sigh. "She is coping Keenan. As best as she can. Thankfully she has her work and she has her friends."

Silence this time on my end. My pulse quickened with just the thought of her.

"She asked about you." He stated quietly. "She wants to know if you are happy. Are you Keenan…are you finally happy?"

I knew there was more to the question than what was being stated. He wasn't asking just for Toni's benefit. He needed to know if I had let her go so he could pursue her. Pursue life with her. There was no easy answer. My love for him wanted him to be happy. My love for her wanted the same thing. Even if her happiness didn't include being with me. But my selfishness could not allow me to think of them being together. I loved her too much. There was no way that I could accept him loving her. Not the way she and I once loved. Not in the ways that I once loved her. My heart couldn't bear it. So if what he was really seeking was validation, he wouldn't get that from me. Not today, probably not ever.

"I can't answer that Kyle."

"You can't or you won't?" A trace of anger now laced his voice. Absently I ran my hands over my face. Today had been a good day. This conversation was threatening to taint it. I looked up just as Sarai opened the door to coffee shop. She gave me a questioning look and I held up one finger to indicate that I wouldn't be much longer. She walked back inside.

"What do you want from me Kyle? You want my permission to love her? I can't give you that. I won't accept that."

"Your permission?" His voice rose. "I don't need your permission to love her. I have been loving her long before you came to Atlanta. And let's remember that you damn sure didn't feel the need to get my permission."

My own body was becoming tense with anger and frustration. He couldn't put this on me. If he loved her, he should have stepped up when he had the opportunity. But he didn't. He let me love her and that couldn't be undone. That's on him.

"Kyle, I have loved you like my brother. Trust me when I say that I'm sorry about this situation with Toni. But I *love* her. Regardless of whether or not I'm with her. I love her man."

When he spoke again, the anger had dissipated. There was only resignation left. "I do know that Keenan, I know. But *I* love her."

I hung up the phone without as much of a goodbye. My life was in turmoil. I looked towards the door of the coffee shop. Inside was the woman who bore the title of my wife. The mother of my child. The woman who has known me and loved me for ten years. In Atlanta, was the woman who loves me as if she has known me a lifetime. Just a few short moments ago I was prepared to move forward. Yet, making that choice would not only mean losing Toni, but leaving Kyle to pick up the pieces. This was that point of no return. No matter the choice, there would be destruction. Walking towards the door, preparing myself to face Sarai, I had no choice but to face the question that would ultimately change my life: Was I in or was I out?

Note to the Reader:

I sincerely appreciate your purchase of my book. I certainly hope that you enjoyed it. Please let others know about your experience. For independent authors, getting our art into the hands of the masses truly takes a grassroots effort. My art, my words, are my purpose. Thank you for being a part of my journey.

LAKINIA RAMSEY is a native of Sumter County, Georgia. She was raised as an Army "brat." She has an MBA from Georgia Southwestern State University. She has worked as a case manager for DFCS (Department of Family and Children Services), an Outreach Coordinator and Legal Advocate for domestic violence victims, a Program Coordinator for the Victim Witness Assistance Program (Southwestern Judicial Circuit) and a Program Specialist for the Georgia Crime Victims Compensation Program. Previous works include "More Than a Coffee Pot" (Yahoo Contributor Network) and work as a freelance writer, editor, and web content creator. She is the Co-Founder of Abstract Village (An organization for the promotion of creativity and art). "Good Intentions" is her first novel. Upcoming projects include a second novel and a book of poetry.

"Good Intentions"

Reader's Guide

1. What is your overall opinion of the book?

2. What do you think about the plot? Did the story pull you in; did you feel that you had to force yourself to read the book?

3. How do you feel about the characters? Were they realistic? Do you think they were well developed?

4. How do the characters change or evolve throughout the course of the story? What events trigger such changes?

5. In the book, the main characters both make decisions that have moral implications. How do you feel about their choices? Do you think you would have made the same or different decisions?

6. What specific themes occur throughout the book? What point/s do you think the author is trying to get across to the reader?

7. What is the setting? Does it come to life? Does it enhance the story? Did you feel you were experiencing the time and place in which the book was set?

8. Did the book end the way you expected?

9. Would you recommend this book to other readers?

58005680R00124

Made in the USA
Columbia, SC
17 May 2019